Courtney's gaze traveled over Jonas's hand where it lay on his stomach, just touching his belt.

Lean fingers, the same ones he'd spread across her back. Jonas's hands made her think about fingertips brushing over bare skin. About heat and light.

A crash like the sound of metal on metal brought her mind flying back to the present. Her feet hit the floor as she sat up and stared through the doorway to the back of the house.

She leaned over with her upper body resting on Jonas's thighs. "Wake up."

"What?" The sleepiness hadn't faded from his voice.

"I hear something."

His eyes popped open. "Where?"

"Out back, upstairs. I don't really kn⟨ow⟩."

He eased her off him and ⟨...⟩g his feet into the sneakers he ⟨...⟩

He stood u⟨p⟩ ⟨...⟩the floor and a gun ⟨...⟩r felt safer.

sat up, slipping

e felt by the couch.

p in a fluid movement, feet on

in his hand. Courtney had never

HelenKay Dimon

WHEN SHE WASN'T LOOKING

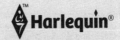
Harlequin®

TORONTO NEW YORK LONDON
AMSTERDAM PARIS SYDNEY HAMBURG
STOCKHOLM ATHENS TOKYO MILAN MADRID
PRAGUE WARSAW BUDAPEST AUCKLAND

To Alison Kent for keeping me sane
every day with your emails.

Recycling programs
for this product may
not exist in your area.

ISBN-13: 978-0-373-69619-2

WHEN SHE WASN'T LOOKING

ABOUT THE AUTHOR

Award-winning author HelenKay Dimon spent twelve years in the most unromantic career ever—divorce lawyer. After dedicating all that effort to helping people terminate relationships, she is thrilled to deal in happy endings and write romance novels for a living. Now her days are filled with gardening, writing, reading and spending time with her family in and around San Diego. HelenKay loves hearing from readers, so stop by her website, www.helenkaydimon.com, and say hello.

Books by HelenKay Dimon

HARLEQUIN INTRIGUE

CAST OF CHARACTERS

Jonas Porter—A former officer with the Drug Enforcement Agency (DEA) in Los Angeles, who leaves the city and unwanted publicity behind for a calmer life as the deputy police chief in a coastal Oregon town. Then he meets Courtney and an easy assignment turns into a desperate bid to protect her and figure out who wants her dead.

Courtney Allen—She's a woman trying to live a quiet existence under a new name across the country from her old life, but her horrifying past keeps chasing her. She's accustomed to running and working alone, but Jonas is not an easy man to ignore…or leave.

Cade Willis—He shares a difficult past with Courtney. Like her, he has reinvented himself. But he's not satisfied. He's now using his contacts to track down Courtney and his decisions have far-reaching effects. Is he a victim or the killer Courtney fears?

Kurt Handler—The powerful businessman has spent his life protecting his family and their security. He was there for Courtney when she lost everything all those years ago. He's back in her life again, and danger seems to follow him.

Walt Roberts—He is Jonas's mentor and the county sheriff. He helped Jonas land his current law enforcement position and doesn't want to see him lose it. The biggest problem is that Walt doesn't trust Courtney, but the question is whether Walt can be trusted.

Richmond Tobin—Jonas's best friend. When Jonas needs trusted backup, Rich is the guy. He's trustworthy and strong, but nothing in the case is what it seems.

Chapter One

Jonas Porter yawned as he marched up the front porch steps to the Craftsman-style bungalow in the middle of nowhere. At ten in the morning he'd been on shift for more than sixteen straight hours, thanks to the Webber kid taking his neighbor's car for a joyride that ended with a big splash into the Siuslaw River.

When he took the law-enforcement position, Jonas had been promised relative peace and quiet by the county sheriff and Jonas's longtime mentor, Walt Roberts. Since Jonas needed a break and crime didn't run rampant in Aberdeen, the small Oregon town where the river dumped into the Pacific Ocean, the job looked like the perfect solution. If a drunk preteen with a lack of common sense turned out to be the biggest problem, Jonas could live with that.

Agreeing to handle one small task on his way back to his place to pass out was probably not his brightest move. He needed sleep, but this should be easy. In and out, and then he could slip into bed for a few hours.

He knocked on the dark red door. The rock beat thumping inside and shaking the walls cut off. He double-checked the house number to make sure he was at the right place. He expected an older lady, a grandmother type. He guessed this one liked her music loud, which blew his older-woman stereotype apart.

In the resulting silence he waited for someone to open up. When no one did, he raised his hand to try again and nearly punched the woman who threw the door open.

"Sorry," he mumbled as he stared into big brown eyes filled with a wariness that appeared older than the rest of her.

"Yes?" Her smile faded when her gaze traveled down his chest.

A guy could get a complex. "Ma'am, is this your house?"

"Of course."

The high cheekbones and slim figure didn't make any sense. Young and pretty with shoulder-length brown hair, and not at all the lonely older woman he'd been told to check on. This one couldn't be more than in her mid to late twenties. She wore a slim, long-sleeved red T-shirt and, if his guess was right, no bra.

He pretended not to notice the last part. "I'm Lieutenant Jonas Porter, the deputy police chief."

"I got that much from the uniform and name tag."

"Uh, right. Sure." She had him stuttering like the Webber kid.

"Why are you here?" She wiped her hands on her olive cargo pants but didn't shift one inch to let him in.

Young or old, she hardly struck him as a woman who needed police assistance to make sure she took her medicine on time. This one could handle her business without any help from him. The flat line of her mouth and clenched fists suggested she wanted to kick him right off the porch.

"We had a call," he explained. "I'm here for a wellness check."

Something flashed in her dark eyes. "What are you talking about?"

"Your husband has been trying to reach you and when you couldn't—"

Her grip tightened on the door. "My husband?"

"Yes, ma'am. My understanding is that he's away from home on business." When she continued to stare at him with that you've-lost-your-mind expression, Jonas tried again. "He called a friend who called the police in Maryland who contacted my office. I'm here as a courtesy."

"Maryland?"

Seemed she had a repetition problem. "Yes, ma'am. Your husband was worried you'd forgotten to take your medications."

"You think I need drugs?"

Jonas refused to be thrown off stride. "Your husband said something about a bad fall recently."

"Is this a joke?"

That was what Jonas was starting to wonder. "No, ma'am."

"You obviously have the wrong person." She started to close the door. Right in his face.

He caught the edge with one hand as the other went to the top of his gun. "Hold up."

The move was pure instinct. He'd once waited a second too long and vowed never to make that mistake again.

She didn't miss the move. Her gaze zipped to his weapon. "Excuse me?"

"Let's calm down for a second and walk through this."

"Do I look nervous to you?"

"Actually, yes." Something was wrong here. Very wrong. The request to his office had been clear. The husband had a friend who pulled some strings. This type of thing didn't happen all the time, but it *did* happen.

This had to be the place. Right number. Right street. The description fit right down to the colors of the flowers in the pot next to the door.

Jonas took a deep breath and doubled back to try a new angle. "You are Margaret Taynor, correct?"

Her face paled. She looked as if all the blood drained from her upper body.

Yeah, definitely something wrong here. "Ma'am?"

She shook her head as her throat moved in a hard swallow. "No."

"That wasn't a very convincing answer."

"It's not my name."

If he hadn't been paying attention he might have missed them, but she showed some of the classic signs of deception—no eye contact, shallow breathing and the skin color that came right before someone threw up on his shoes. She dodged questions and gave half answers.

"If there's a problem between you and your husband, I might be able to help."

"No." She blew out a few breaths.

Jonas didn't know what to believe, but the pieces sure didn't fit. The wellness-check request didn't match the person in front of him. This woman did not recently fall down and break her hip. Her biggest problem, as far as he could see, was with telling the truth.

He wanted to know what was really going on. "If you're more comfortable talking to a female officer, I can—"

She waved a hand in front of her face. "I meant that, no, I am not Margaret Taynor."

"Yeah, you said that."

"Then are we done here?"

As if he could walk away now and still deserve to wear the badge. "Ma'am, enough with the verbal games. Who are you exactly?"

She stared past him, out to the tree-lined road and the mountains surrounding her place. "Does that matter?"

He shifted so his back wasn't quite as exposed. At this angle, he could swing around and aim for the yard or the house if he had to. "Actually, I think it does."

She nibbled on her lip. "Courtney Allen."

"And you live here?"

"Yes."

"Anyone else?"

She edged the door tighter against her side and one step closer to shutting him out. "I don't have a husband or a clue what you're talking about."

Jonas slipped his shoe into the space between the door and the frame, though he doubted she'd think twice of breaking a few bones if she had to.

"Do you know Margaret Taynor?" he asked.

Courtney glanced at his shoe then let her gaze wander up his body nice and slow, as if weighing her chances of running. He'd seen it before. This was the second before panic gave way to stupid.

"We're done here," she said.

He reassessed. Not domestic violence. Maybe some criminal activity in her past. Something she hadn't settled. "You want me to come back with a warrant?"

"If you think you have probable cause, go ahead and try."

The woman knew her legal lingo. He took that as a sign she either watched a lot of television or had some personal experience in this area. "Ma'am, I think you should come with me."

Her shoulders straightened. It was as if she grew two inches just by standing there. "And I think you should move your foot before you lose it."

Wanting to see what she would do, he slid it back. "Fair enough."

"Goodbye, Officer." She slammed the door before he could say anything else.

So much for going off duty.

COURTNEY GLANCED through the peephole and saw the officer still standing on her porch. The guy had black hair, broad shoulders and an attitude that spelled trouble.

But she had bigger problems than a six-foot-something guy with a gun. Margaret Taynor? Oh, she knew Margaret. Courtney also knew if someone was asking, he'd finally found her.

With practiced quiet steps, she jogged to the back door and peeked out. The officer hadn't slipped around to this side of the house. That meant she had time, probably seconds only, but she'd memorized the plan long ago.

She had to run.

She'd picked a house on this street on purpose. The neighborhood sat on the edge of Siuslaw National Forest. The lush woods behind the quiet property provided the perfect protection and the easiest escape.

She'd never been one for luck, but today she had it. Low wind and the rain from the night before had cleared. A crisp, sunny spring day beamed in through her kitchen window.

She eased the door open, scanning the open backyard for unwanted visitors. Branches from two trees bent over, forming a makeshift arch and beckoning her to the far end of her property. A tall fence outlined the yard. Nothing stood between her and safety. From here it was a dead run to the far gate.

If she kept quiet, Officer Tall, Dark and Dangerous wouldn't hear her. That was the hope. He could waste time fiddling with his radio and she could run.

She held the door with two fingers to keep it from banging shut behind her. Two steps down and she hit the grass. Her cheap sneakers slid in the oozing mud, but she stayed on her feet. Air pounded in her lungs and a soft breeze whipped through her hair as she ran.

She lunged for the gate and flipped the cover open on the small security box. A car key fell into her hand as her fingers typed in the code. After a click the outside alarm shut off.

With one last glance over her shoulder, she said a silent goodbye to the only place that had felt like home in years. The pain of leaving ripped through her with the force of a blade. Her stomach dropped and her heart ached. She'd finally started to build memories, enjoy her work. She'd even made a real friend. She'd felt free to live again.

But her brain knew those days were over. Running was the right decision. If she stayed, she'd die like the rest of them.

Swallowing back the tears she refused to let fall, she opened the gate…and ran straight into the broad chest of Lieutenant Trouble.

Jonas grabbed her upper arms and held her a few inches away from him. "Hello."

Her voice deserted her. "Uh-huh."

"Going somewhere?"

Her breath rushed out of her lungs and refused to come back. "No."

He smiled. "Good answer."

Chapter Two

The woman with the truth problem tried to wiggle out of Jonas's hold. "You have to let me go."

"Not going to happen." With his patience expired, he shot her his best I'm-done-here glare.

"I haven't done anything wrong." The tension over her shoulders eased. She switched from fighting to boneless.

But he wasn't ready to trust her, so he held on. "From my experience, innocent people don't run."

"You're kind of big to be that naive."

"Sounds like you have trust issues, but—" He reached for his radio. In that brief span where his fingers didn't wrap around her arm, she took off. "You've got to be kidding. You're running?"

She crossed over the gravel road separating the back of her private property from the protected forest behind. Turning to the left, she slipped along the fence running parallel to the tree line. Not once did she look back.

The great escape took all of two seconds and left him staring in reluctant admiration. At least he wasn't alone in his cluelessness. He realized she actually believed she could pull this off.

"Margaret…" He searched his brain for the name she'd used and shouted that one even louder. "Courtney."

When she didn't stop, he took off after her. He could stay

still and aim, call out a warning then hit the ground right near her with a shot. The move would scare the crap out of her, but he decided not to play it that way.

He ran behind her, gaining on her and closing the distance with each step. Years of training, all those physical-fitness tests, served him well. At thirty-three he still ran a seven-minute mile.

Shame he hated running so much.

He'd almost reached her when her sneakers skidded on the loose stones and she dashed to the right. She headed for a small cutout in the fence where two poles met and only a slip of space waited. With a quick glance over her shoulder, she turned sideways and shimmied her way through the impossibly small hole.

"Courtney!" He grabbed her foot but she kicked out, sliding out of his grasp as she tumbled back.

A knee buckled but she stayed on her feet. With a push-off from her hand against the ground, she took off again. His string of profanity didn't stop her any better than the yelling had.

He held the poles and tried to figure out an easy way in. His shoulders wouldn't even fit in the space, which meant he had to go over.

I should have shot at her when I had the chance.

The metal clanked as he moved down the fence line a few feet and curved his fingers through the chain links. Ignoring the rough edges slicing into his palms, he pulled his body up and over the twelve-foot fence.

By the time his feet hit the wet ground on the other side, she was gone. Not that hiding would save her. No, he was in this now. All traces of exhaustion and thoughts of sleep left his head. He would catch her, take her in and probably issue a lecture or two in the process.

She didn't strike him as a hard-edged criminal, but she

was starting to act like one. From his experience, there was only one way to catch someone determined to flee—rough and fast.

Taking turns keeping watch behind him and sweeping his gaze over the landscape in front of him, he stalked through the woods. The towering trees blocked the sun, letting only pools of light filter through. With his back against a tree, he scanned the area. A flash of red moved up ahead to his left.

Found her.

His steps quiet and firm on the slippery ground, he swung out wide, racing to her far side and hoping to come up behind her. He could see her in a clearing. Her arms never stopped working as she reached over an outcropping of rocks. She didn't do anything to hide the crunching of sticks beneath her feet or her deep breathing.

Weapon close by, he shifted into the open area. Ahead of her a dirt road lead out and curved deeper into the forest. This close he could see he read the situation wrong. She wasn't standing by rocks. She tugged on a large piece of tan canvas, a cloth that had blended into the landscape only a few seconds before.

Her gaze darted around, checking the area behind her but ignoring the rest of the woods. With a loud thwack, she snapped the material to the side before throwing it to the ground.

"You have a car out here?" He spoke before his brain clicked into gear.

The sunlight glinted off the metal in her hand when she spun around. "How did you—"

"And a gun. A car and a gun. How enterprising of you, Ms. Courtney Allen, or whatever your name really is." He watched the weapon shake in her fingers and judged the chance of knocking her down without getting a bullet through his forehead.

"It's Courtney."

He snorted. "And why would I not believe you?"

"It's not what you think."

"What was your earlier comment about being innocent? Last I checked innocent people don't have an escape plan."

"I told you to leave me alone."

"Yeah, that's not going to happen now. I can't have a woman racing around my jurisdiction with two names and a gun."

His impression of her kept changing. He'd read her as a victim originally, but she sure seemed ready to pull the trigger now.

"I haven't done anything wrong." Her voice wavered on the words as her chest rose and fell.

"Threatening a police officer, resisting arrest, and I'm betting you don't have a license for that." He nodded in the direction of the gun leveled at him from a distance of less than ten feet.

"Do you think I care about a license?"

"What I want is for both of us to live through the next few minutes. The best way to make that happen is for you to lower your weapon." He pressed his hand down, trying to get her to follow his lead and drop the damn thing. "You put it down, we talk and this whole misunderstanding goes away."

Her gaze darted to the left then back to him. "It's not safe."

Since he was looking down the barrel of a gun, he had to agree with her on that one. "I have a good office, quiet and private. We can talk there. Work this out."

"I'm leaving."

"We both are." He started lifting his hand to his shoulder then stopped when she stepped closer, her finger inching toward certain death for him.

"Don't move."

"Wait a second. I'm just trying to show you my radio. I called for backup."

Her arms tensed to the point of snapping. "When?"

Never, actually, but he had no intention of telling her that. "There's nowhere to go."

She shook the weapon at him again. "Drop the radio and the gun."

"Courtney, if I take this gun out, if my fingers get even a quarter-inch closer to the trigger, I'm going to aim it at you. Do you understand that?"

"I do now." She pointed the gun at the car. "Get in."

He'd been expecting surrender, thought maybe she'd even engage in a little smart panic. An offer for a ride took him by surprise.

He forced his mouth in a flat line to keep from giving his shock away. "Excuse me?"

"You're coming with me. I'll drop you off up the road." She nodded her head and repeated the comment, as if getting comfortable with the idea.

That made one of them. "I wouldn't even fit in that car, Courtney."

The vehicle, if that was what it was, looked more like an egg with a steering wheel. With mud and leaves caked to the wheels, he doubted she could even get it to move.

And then there was the part where he wasn't getting in. He gave self-defense presentations all the time and had one very simple rule: do everything you can to not get in a vehicle with your attacker.

She frowned at him. "Your comfort is not my main priority."

"Clearly, but do you really want to add kidnapping to your list of crimes?"

"I want to be able to get a head start. Up the road a bit,

you'll get out and the radio will stay with me. By the time someone picks you up or you get out of the forest, I'll be long gone." She ticked off the specs as if she had them memorized.

"Sounds like you've had this plan brewing for a long time."

"You have ten seconds." She started walking, backing her way toward the car before bracing her shoulders against the door.

The move took away the option of wrestling her to the ground, or at least made it harder. "Or?"

"I'm going to shoot you."

"I doubt that," he said, even as he believed the opposite was possible at this point.

"I have nothing to lose. Do you really want to test me?" She whispered the words but they echoed through the woods with the force of a fierce shake.

He read the desperation in her eyes. Worry and fear showed in the tight lines of her face. People pushed to the edge often did dumb things. Add in a weapon and the chance for idiocy tripled.

At this range, she'd likely hit some part of his body, and he had quite a few he wasn't ready to lose just yet. That left only one or two options, none of them good. He could draw his weapon, likely get off a shot before she knew what hit her. He could rush her and risk a bullet. Even if he hit her, one or both of them would get hurt.

Or he could wait it out as he tried to figure out who she was and what had her so willing to throw her life away to get out of Aberdeen. The curious part of him wanted to go with the latter. Something about her had him intrigued. Probably had something to do with this being the first time he stood on the wrong side of a gun held by a woman. He'd had plenty of males shoot at him, men and boys, but she was the first female.

He lifted his hand away from his gun and raised his palms in the air. "My shift is over, by the way. I should be at home sleeping."

She shrugged. "You're the one who came to my door."

The woman has an answer for everything. "And believe me when I say I regret that."

"Drop the radio on the ground and kick it to me."

Rather than debate, he unclipped it from his shoulder and threw it at her feet. When she smashed her heel into the speaker and kicked the broken shell into the thick underbrush to her left, he winced.

"Was that necessary?"

"Yes. Now the gun," she ordered.

No way was he giving up his weapon. Didn't matter that he had another one at his ankle and a small knife at the ready in his back pocket. Getting disarmed by a hundred twenty pounds of lady trouble was not on his daily agenda. "I told you what would happen if I touched it."

"I can't trust you not to pull it on me in the car."

"True." He took a step toward her. "But I could have drawn numerous times during the last half hour and didn't. I've decided to ride this out. Until you give me reason to think otherwise, I'm content to keep the gun in the holster."

The seconds ticked by. With the rustle of branches and squawking of birds, the sounds of the forest surrounded them. Neither of them moved.

When the human silence threatened to blanket them, she opened the passenger-side door with a creak and put one foot inside. "Go around and get in, but keep those hands in the air."

"I'm driving?"

"Unless you want to ride in the trunk."

He followed her gaze to the back end of the car. He doubted he could get a leg in there. Next thing she'd suggest tying him to the roof.

He opened one hand. "Keys?"

She reached into her pants and pulled out a single key. "Thought you'd pick that option."

"You mean you hoped I would."

She threw the key. "That, too."

Chapter Three

Courtney's arms ached from holding the gun. The small car bounced as they drove over deep divots and through holes filled with yesterday's rain.

The bumps vibrated through her. Her head whipped from side to side, and her body fell back against the seat. In an attempt to stay steady, she braced her foot on the floor and faced him. Her muscles burned as the weight of the metal in her hands sapped all her strength. So did the mind-numbing terror flowing through her at a speed that threatened to choke her.

She'd been on the run in one form or another since she was seventeen, so that part wasn't new. Being found, having an armed police officer track her and even now be close enough to take her down, added a new layer of anxiety to her already convoluted life. After logging in hours at the shooting range, she knew how to use the gun, but pointing it at another human being, someone other than her intended target, turned out to be harder than she expected.

"What's the plan here?" Jonas shifted his gaze between her and the old running trail they bumbled over on their getaway.

He'd been right about the tight fit. His hair brushed against the roof and his shoulders swallowed up his seat and part of hers. The way he doubled over the steering wheel only made his driving worse.

"I told you," she said.

His handcuffs and baton rolled around at her feet where she'd thrown them minutes before, but his hands stayed on the wheel. "Right. The dump-the-guy-with-a-badge scheme."

"Would you rather I shoot you?"

"There's probably a middle ground."

"If you say so." She pointed. "Take the road to the left."

He leaned in close enough to the front window to press his nose against the glass. "You see a road?"

"Right here!" Her teeth rattled as he hit the brakes and the car shuddered underneath her. She grabbed on to the back of the seat and saw his gaze bounce to her gun, which only made her hold it tighter. "The rangers use it for emergencies."

"Guess that explains how you hid the car."

"I moved it every few days to keep hikers from uncovering and reporting it. Many folks out here complain about the trash in the forest and organize groups to go out and pick it up. Imagine what they'd do about a car."

"I'm impressed with your preplanning." He exhaled. "Now tell me why you think it's necessary."

She guessed his goal was to throw her off, but the quick change in conversation didn't work. She'd lived with her secrets and researched in the quiet darkness long enough not to lose control that easily.

When she didn't immediately respond, he snapped a finger. "Any chance I could get an answer?"

"Evil."

His gaze stayed on her for an extra second this time. "Is that a first or last name?"

"You think this is funny?"

His foot eased off the gas and they sputtered to a stop as

he faced her. "No, Courtney. I think you're in big trouble and it's getting worse with every decision you make."

"You don't know anything about me or my life."

"The way I see it you have two choices."

She could only see one: hide until she figured out who killed her family and why.

She cleared her throat, trying to wipe out the debilitating emotion that always poured through her when she thought about them. "You're going to go over this hill then cut to the left. And I mean fast. If you hesitate, we'll hit a tree."

"Good to know." He hit the gas and the car chugged along the rough road.

Something in his light tone made her smile. "You won't see it until—"

"What is that?"

She turned to see what had him swearing. "I don't see—"

"Where did he come from?" Jonas's hands tightened on the wheel. As he started shouting, his knuckles turned white.

She watched in horror as a truck with a huge front grill barreled right at them on her side of the car. It appeared out of nowhere, gobbling up branches and dragging them under its tires.

She sat down hard in the seat facing forward and dropped the gun to the floor. With her arms locked, she balanced her palms against the dashboard. "Move!"

"I see it."

"He's going to hit us."

"Get down!" Jonas turned the wheel sharp to the left. The car bobbled as tires spun, kicking up mud and squealing in protest.

Just as the traction grabbed, the truck smashed into the back passenger side. Metal crunched as the doors crashed in and the roof buckled with an earsplitting thunk. Her body rocked in her seat until the belt dug deep into her skin.

Pain raced up her arm as she watched Jonas struggle to keep the car upright. Then the world spun around her. Her stomach rolled in time with the car when it turned over. She screamed until she lost her breath.

When the rocking stopped, she lifted her hands and they fell until they hung in front of her. The dashboard pressed up against her knees and her vision blurred, cutting in and out. Something clicked in her neck when she turned to look at Jonas. His eyes were closed with his arms bent underneath him. Blood covered his eye and ran along his forehead.

They were upside down.

His first name floated through her mind. "Jonas?"

She whispered through a scratchy throat just as footsteps thudded around her. She couldn't make out the direction, but her stomach plummeted at the sound.

She closed her eyes and when she opened them again, a face popped up outside the broken window next to Jonas's head. A scream raced through her but she swallowed it. "Who…who are you?"

The man with the blond military-cut hair and chin stubble smiled. Feral heat radiated off him. "It's time to go."

"Why?" She felt underneath her stomach for the abandoned gun. Stretching out her hands, she touched it but it danced off her fingertips.

The man smacked his hand against what used to be the bottom of the car. "You're worth a lot of money, and I intend to collect."

"I can't move." She looked at Jonas's holster—empty— then her gaze skipped to his face. His eyes were open. Dark and furious he stared at her. She tried to read the look and decided he needed time. She focused on the attacker. "I think I'm injured."

"You can slide out or I can come get you."

The attacker's words skidded across her nerves, leaving an icy trail in their wake. "Give me a second."

In a blur, Jonas moved. He brought his gun up in a flowing arc. At the last second he lifted his head and shot right out the window without aiming. One second the attacker hovered there, leering. The next leaves rustled and red sprayed across the broken glass. The only sound was the lone beep as Jonas's elbow hit the horn when his arm flopped back down.

The whole thing took a second but moved in a slow motion that played more like hours. She'd never been a big fan of the police, but she was grateful for Jonas.

"Is that guy dead?" she asked.

Jonas rubbed his head and came away with a hand stained with blood. "Hurt or not, I don't miss from this range."

"I guess that's a yes." The horror of death washed over her. The man, whoever he was, died because of her. "I can't believe this."

"Courtney." Jonas's husky voice broke through the screaming in her brain. "Are you okay?"

Her hands shook hard enough to bang against the dashboard. "You're bleeding."

"It's minor."

She touched her fingers to his forehead and trembled against his skin as the haze settled over his eyes. "We have to get out of here. Can you move?"

Reaching down, he unclipped his seat belt and his body slumped closer to the ground. "I can't make it out of this window at this angle. We need to rock."

"What?"

"Try to tip the car on its side." He shifted and his eyes closed.

"Jonas."

His eyes popped back open. His forehead creased. He

didn't yell or complain, but the muscles in his cheeks tightened. "I'm okay."

"I can get out." She had no idea if that was true. The seat pinned her knees under her, and the numbness in her right shoulder had spread down to her fingertips.

"Any chance you have a phone?" he asked.

"No, and for the record I'm sorry I chucked your radio into the trees."

His mouth kicked up on one side. "Makes two of us."

"I can slip out—" She hissed when her weight shifted to her thigh and a string of pain ran down to her feet.

"Don't move until we know what's wrong with you."

"We can't stay here."

"We won't." He used his elbow to knock out the rest of the window's broken glass. With his upper body outside the car up to his armpit, he reached for something outside.

He let out a long, growling yell, then fell back against the steering wheel. His chest lifted on harsh breaths. With eyes closed and sweat streaking across his eyebrows, he locked his jaw and sat still.

She recognized pain when she saw it. "What are you—"

"I can do it." This time he threw his body to the side, lifting farther out of his seat. His hand slapped against the ground before it disappeared. When he flopped back he had something in his hand and held it under her nose. "Here."

She stared at the cell phone and realized Jonas picked it off the attacker. "How did you know he had one?"

"Lucky guess." Jonas gasped between breaths. "At some point he'd have to be able to call the person paying him to grab you."

"Smart."

"I'm sure it's a pay-as-you-go and won't trace back to anyone, but at least we have it."

"So, you believe me." The words were heavy in her mouth, hard to say and even harder to accept.

"Call 911."

She turned the phone over in her hands. The plan involved running, not hanging around to talk with the police. And if Jonas decided to file charges...

"Courtney." Strength returned to his voice for that one word.

But common sense returned on a rush. She shook her head. "I have to leave first."

"You're hurt. Hell, *I'm* hurt."

Guilt ate at her, but she ignored it. "You know I was telling the truth, that I can't stay. Someone is after me."

"Running isn't the answer."

"It's worked so far."

He leaned closer to her. "Call and we'll figure out everything else later."

"But I—"

"Just dial." His head lolled to the side. "Please."

She didn't know if it was the pain in his voice or the pleading, but she gave in, threw all rational thought aside and pressed the buttons. On the second ring, she glanced over at him. The color had left his face and his hands opened and closed as if he were trying to keep the blood flowing.

"This is a mistake." Courtney didn't realize she'd said the words out loud until she heard them.

His rough laugh turned into a cough. "At least the day can't get worse."

But she knew better.

Chapter Four

Kurt Handler stared at the closed file on the edge of his desk. He didn't have to open it. He knew every line contained in the four-inch-thick folder. No one else ever read through it or touched it. He carried the pages with him in his briefcase and in his head. The words haunted his nights and hovered over him during the day.

He spun his chair around and stared out the windows lining the wall behind his desk. He'd been watching over this part of Washington, D.C., his small corner of the world with the famous Watergate and Kennedy Center as his neighbors, for a decade.

He earned every square foot of the tenth-floor office space. He put in endless hours, ignoring his sons' baseball games and wife's pleas for more time at home, to focus on his commercial-real-estate business.

His job was to stockpile money and guarantee security for all four of them. Every time the market took a downturn, he adjusted. When his competitors struck, he hit back even harder. He owned huge portions of this city. In an area driven by power, he brokered more deals, negotiated more dollars, than any of the new-money business owners trying to muscle into his territory.

He'd survived and thrived, putting his kids through college and gifting them with trust funds that would ensure they'd never have to struggle or beg as he had. The idea he could lose it all because of the meddling of an ignorant girl made him furious.

She refused to accept the facts in front of her and move on. She insisted the police got it all wrong. She could ruin everything.

He waited for his associate in that craphole of a town in Oregon to check in. Kurt hated depending on someone else for help, but he had hired the best. And if he had to take care of the problem on his own this time, he would.

FIVE HOURS, an ambulance, two police cars and a hydraulic spreader later, Jonas sat on an emergency-room table with his legs dangling over the side and his shoulder bandaged.

They were lucky to be alive. The mangled metal formerly known as a car had crashed around them but not into them. A thousand little things had probably made the difference, but the rough terrain and the crawling speed he was forced to drive had made survival an option.

The hospital loudspeaker spewed a constant stream of announcements. Nurses rushed in and out of the individual cubicles lining the L-shaped room. He heard bells and alarms, smelled the harsh scent of antiseptic.

He blocked it all out and concentrated on everything that had happened since he showed up on Courtney's doorstep that morning. The pieces sat there, but he couldn't put them together in a comprehensible way. Chases, car accidents, killing. Not his favorite way to spend a day.

It all led back to her, to something in her past. It, whatever "it" was, put her in danger and nearly got him killed. He'd figure it out. At the very least he intended to gather more intel before getting into a car with her the next time.

He also vowed not to leave her side until the threat passed. Right now she lay in a bed on the other side of the flimsy curtain. He could hear her grumbling, even had to argue with her a few times when she told him she was ready to leave.

He'd asked the staff to put her in the cubicle at the end of the hall, thinking she'd have to go through him to sneak out. But he wouldn't have been surprised if she slipped through an air-conditioning vent to get away. This woman had a serious running issue.

Richmond Tobin, Jonas's first friend in Aberdeen and a fellow police officer, walked in. He stood six feet and had wrestled in college. Six years out, he looked as if he could battle a train and come out ahead.

"You're supposed to be lying down. You know, resting," he said.

"Tell me about it." Jonas rolled his shoulders and had to fight back the wave of nausea that hit him right behind the pain.

"Brought a change of clothes and your cell, just as you requested." Rich dumped a gym bag next to Jonas's thigh and held up a gun. "Also managed to liberate your weapon."

Jonas took it, ran his finger across the side before checking it, then slipped it and his holster onto his belt. "Bet the nurses loved that."

"I flashed my badge and reminded them you were in charge since the police chief retired, so it was all your responsibility."

Jonas saw mounds of paperwork and a meeting with the town council in his future. "Thanks for that."

"While you're at it, care to tell me how you got stuck in the middle of the forest with a dead body next to you?" Rich fell into the seat across from Jonas. "Someone I have to identify, I might add."

"Long story."

"Then there's the woman who isn't elderly or in need of a wellness check."

"Yeah. Courtney."

Rich's eyes widened. "You're on a first-name basis?"

"Almost getting killed will do that to a relationship. Speeds things up." For some messed-up reason, she was now Courtney in his head. Jonas knew the informal reference bordered on inappropriate, but he'd worry about that later when he sorted out everything else that had happened that day.

"Uh-huh. And how did all of this happen again?"

Jonas tried to rub the crick out his neck. "You asked about fifty questions in the last two minutes."

"Okay, how about this one?" Rich leaned forward with his elbows on his knees and smiled at his boss. "How did a hundred-pound woman get the drop on you?"

"You're light on the weight, and I threatened him with my gun," Courtney shouted from behind the curtain and over the protests of the nurse who was taking her vital signs.

Rich whistled. "Interesting."

Jonas bit back a groan. He'd hear about this for months. Cops loved this crap. Being the new officer on the squad and the one with the highest rank, the target on his back grew bigger each day. His four-month perfect record blown with one comment from Courtney.

"The dead guy tried to kill her," he said.

Rick pulled his chair closer to the exam table as he lowered his voice. "Any chance we know who or why?"

"Not yet." But Jonas was about to get some of those answers. He hated when people lied to him. Not having all the facts didn't sit any better.

He eased off the table, ignoring the aches thumping through every part of his body. He'd somehow made it through a car flip with only a dislocated shoulder, cut-up knee and bruised ribs.

He'd developed the bad attitude during the ambulance ride.

"Where are you going?" Rich asked.

"I have some questions of my own." Jonas ignored the amusement in his friend's voice and started walking.

The rings jangled on the metal rod and the nurse squealed as Jonas ripped the curtain aside. "You can't be in here," she said in a huff.

At fifty, Nurse Ramsey ran the emergency room with an iron fist. Jonas knew her from the times he brought in suspects and car-accident victims. She did her job and was not even a little impressed by his gun and badge.

Standing there without a shirt but with a weapon strapped to his side, he wished he'd taken a second to get dressed. It was too late now. "I need to speak with Courtney."

Even while lying flat on her back with a tube sticking out of her arm, Courtney rolled her eyes. "You could have just asked."

"I'm calling security." The nurse brushed past Jonas and ran right into Rich.

He flashed a badge. "Since we're the police that probably won't be necessary."

The nurse scowled. "I know who you are, Richmond. My husband was your math teacher in high school, but that doesn't mean you're in charge around here."

Since the hospital sat in the middle of Bartholomew County and just over the Aberdeen city line, her argument held some validity.

Still, Jonas came in and out and often stepped up when surrounding jurisdictions needed help. That should buy him some goodwill. At least he thought so. "I can call Walt, if you want."

"Fine." She took her sweet time staring at each of them before turning on her heel and storming out. "You have five minutes."

"She's always such a joy," Rich said after the nurse huffed off.

"She was doing her job." Courtney pushed up on her elbows and peeked around Jonas. "And you are?"

Jonas wasn't in the mood for long-winded introductions. "Rich, Courtney. And vice versa."

"Hello—"

Jonas stood right next to her and put his hand over her arm and lowered it when she started to raise it for a handshake. "Now, tell me what's going on."

Her gaze fell to his waist. "You have your gun back."

"The radio is still MIA. Go ahead and talk."

Rich snorted. "You really know how to make a person want to open up to you."

Courtney looked from one man to the other. "Someone is after me."

"I got that much." Jonas had the headache as a reminder. "I'm guessing that person used you to get to me."

Somehow he knew this would all be his fault. "How do you figure?"

Her face turned green from neck to nose when she sat up. "Ugh."

"You okay?" With a hand against her lower back, he steadied her. Seeing Rich's raised eyebrow had Jonas letting go before he wanted to.

She wobbled, her head dunking forward before pulling up again. "Not really. Are you?"

He could barely stand up without wanting to spill last night's dinner all over the floor. "I will be once you explain how I'm at fault for everything."

She blew out a long breath. "You came to my house, asking about another woman, and all of a sudden I get run over by a truck. It's an A-plus-B thing."

Jonas and Rich took positions on either side of her bed.

More than once, Rich's gaze dipped from her face to her chest. Jonas didn't like the gawking but he understood it.

Even roughed up with leaves in her hair, there was something about Courtney, or whatever her name really was. Pretty, yes, but there was something deeper. An inner strength he admired, even though it resulted in his getting crushed in a tuna can of a car.

But reluctant respect wasn't enough to take him off task. He needed more answers. "Now would be a good time to tell me if you're really Margaret Taynor."

"I promise I'm not."

Rich raised his hand. "Just want you two to know this conversation isn't making any sense."

"That's because Courtney is forgetting to offer up the details." Jonas frowned at her, hoping she'd get the impression that he was done fooling around. "Someone wants to find you, and I think you know why. Care to share?"

"I think I can answer that." The deep voice came from the hall and had both men spinning.

Ignoring the blinding pain in his shoulder, Jonas had his gun up and ready before the man finished his sentence. "Step back."

"Do not move," Rich said at the same time.

The visitor shook his head. "Gentlemen, lower your weapons."

Late forties, with short salt-and-pepper hair and a black suit and tie. Jonas took in the uniform and perfect posture and came to one conclusion—government. He knew the routine. The guy would flash a badge and start talking in half sentences any second now.

Not that anything about the man intimidated Jonas. He'd dealt with the feds—heck, he'd *been* one in his last job and hadn't been impressed. "I don't think so."

"Now." The guy acted as if issuing an order would work.

"And you are?" Rich asked.

"Paul Eckert." Right on cue, the guy held up his hand

then dipped his fingers into his jacket pocket and pulled out a shiny badge. "FBI."

"How did you get in here?" Jonas refused to lower his weapon. "There are two officers out there with specific instructions not to let anyone back here."

"I'm afraid that's my fault. I brought Agent Eckert." Walt Roberts stepped inside the increasingly small space.

"What are you doing here?" Jonas shook his head. He hadn't expected the Bartholomew County sheriff to show up. Then again, Walt had a way of finding the action and being right in the middle of it. Being sixty with a bum leg did not slow him down all that much.

He'd served in the navy with Jonas's dad decades earlier. The men had a bond that extended to Jonas. Walt's personal reference and not-so-subtle insistence that Jonas relocate to Oregon landed him his current deputy position. He owed Walt for many things. A steady paycheck was only one on the impressive list.

"It's getting pretty crowded in here," Courtney said, as she pushed Jonas aside and looked around her bed.

He had to chuckle at her dry statement. "No kidding."

"Would one or more of you consider putting the weapons away? I've seen enough gunplay for one day." She tugged on Jonas's arm as she said it.

Not being one for surprises, he preferred to keep the gun ready, but in deference to the trembling in her palm, he lowered it. He tried to take his anger level down at the same time.

"What's going on?" Jonas asked.

"When word went out that you were in the hospital and most of your squad was either here checking on you or at the crime scene, I got the call to step in. I was on my way over to check on you when Agent Eckert's office made contact."

Walt turned to their suited guest. "So, I brought him along. He pretty much insisted on it."

"I still don't understand what's happening or why the FBI is here," Courtney said.

Eckert stared at her. "It's a serious law-enforcement issue."

Tension exploded in the room. Jonas couldn't breathe without choking on it. And he worried the woman next to him was the cause of it all. "Anything you want to tell me?"

Her entire face fell. Mouth, eyes, everything pulled flat. "I didn't do anything wrong."

"You say that a lot." He turned to the agent. "Eckert?"

"I'd have to disagree with her assessment."

Of course he did. Jonas wondered if this day would ever end. "And why is that?"

"She's under arrest."

Chapter Five

Courtney's painkiller wore off with a hard smack. "What?"

She'd never done anything to attract the attention of the police. If she went the rest of her days without seeing or hearing about another cop, she'd be fine. History taught her to be wary and keep her distance. The whole "run to a policeman if you're in trouble" motto turned her blood icy cold.

Her glance moved to Jonas. Tall, dark, handsome and deadly sarcastic. He had everything she found attractive in a guy...except the badge. She had no choice but to believe in him right now, but at the first opportunity she'd be gone.

Jonas lowered his gun as he stared down the agent. "Where is it?"

The other man's glare telegraphed how little he appreciated being dressed down by a small-town cop. "Excuse me?"

"I want to see the paper."

She had no idea what Jonas was talking about, but the agent didn't blink. Courtney wrote the whole scene off as cop talk, as she scanned the cubicle for an obvious escape route.

Eckert edged closer to the end of the bed. "I need to talk with Ms. Allen alone."

Jonas shook his head. "Not going to happen."

"I agree." She decided Jonas could act the hero on this one with her full support.

Being talked about like a piece of furniture ticked her off, but going with a guy from the FBI terrified her. She'd take anger over fear any day. Fury fueled her, and she would use that energy now to get out of this room.

Eckert held his badge and tapped it against his open palm with a steady thump. His glare switched to her. "You are wanted for questioning—"

One minute she looked into Eckert's face with his lip curled in disgust. The next, Jonas blocked her view. She hadn't seen him move or heard his footsteps, but his broad shoulders now stood as a wall between her and the guy who wanted to take her to jail.

"So then you don't actually have an arrest warrant," Jonas said.

The agent dropped his badge back into his pocket. "Look, Officer—"

"It's Deputy Porter."

"Are you going to interrupt me every time I talk?"

"Possibly."

Walt held up his hands. "Let's calm down here."

Jonas ignored the older man and focused on the agent. "What are you saying she did?"

"This is not a group interview," Eckert said. "I need to speak with Ms. Allen alone."

She put her hand on Jonas's forearm. "Can I refuse?"

Walt shook his head. "You shouldn't."

Jonas's gaze never wavered. He kept all that intensity funneled at the agent. Courtney vowed to keep her mental shield up, but she had to admit Jonas's protective nature sent her stomach flipping.

"Someone tried to kill Ms. Allen a few hours ago," he said. "That same person tried to kill me. So until I know what is going on, she stays with me."

"I think we can agree I'm not a threat to her." Eckert

looked around the room. When no one backed down or nodded in agreement, he blew out a long breath. "Or maybe we can't."

Rich slipped into the seat next to her bed. "We're all law enforcement. You can talk in front of us."

"Fine. Embezzlement." Eckert dropped his verbal bomb and stopped talking.

The longer the silence stretched, the more Jonas's eyes narrowed. "What?"

The word blurred in Courtney's brain. She felt her jaw drop and her eyes bulge. "By me?"

Eckert took out a small notebook and started reading. "Your husband—"

"Again with the husband thing." A rough scream rumbled up her throat but she pushed it back. She settled for throwing up her hands and talking through clenched teeth. "For the last time, I am not now nor have I ever been married."

Eckert's mouth opened and closed twice before any words came out. "That's not possible."

Jonas snorted. "I had the same reaction. The Margaret Taynor thing doesn't make any sense."

It was Eckert's turn to scowl. His gaze bounced around the room. "Who is Margaret Taynor?"

"Isn't that who you're here for?" Jonas asked.

"No." Some of the venom left Eckert's voice. "Are you Courtney Allen?"

"Yes."

Rich tapped on the bed railing next to her head. "So, you have two names but no husband?"

She let her head fall back onto the pillow. It felt good to close her eyes for two seconds. Without a break, her brain might explode.

When she lifted her head again, control had returned. All

those years of practice came rushing back and she pushed out the pain. "You all have the wrong woman."

"Your husband, Peter Allen, has been indicted. He implicated you…" Eckert stared at her. "What now?"

Her face heated to boiling. Another name from her past, another reminder of all she'd lost. Allen Peters, Peter Allen. It couldn't be a coincidence, not so close to having the name Margaret Taynor thrown in her face.

The small corner of normalcy Courtney held on to slipped away. "This can't be happening."

"Do you know Peter Allen?" Jonas's body stiffened and his voice strained as he asked the question.

Fighting back the bile churning in her stomach, she answered with the technical truth. "No."

"Why is everyone in here?" Nurse Ramsey shoved her way back to the bed. The head-shaking and finger-pointing started a second later. "Absolutely not. This is an emergency room. One blood relative at a time. That's it. The rest of you all have to go."

Jonas broke eye contact with Courtney and blinked a few times. "Walt, would you mind taking Agent Eckert here and see what information you can gather?"

Courtney owed the nurse. Darkness had filled the air and blanketed the area. It sucked all the life out of Courtney, made her want to run and not look back.

"I'm not leaving." Eckert crossed his arms over his chest as if to highlight his refusal.

"Are you going to disobey Nurse Ramsey here?" Rich smiled as he asked the question.

"No, he's not." The nurse got in front of Eckert and started pushing him into the hallway. She pinned Jonas with an over-the-shoulder glare. "You may stay but not on account of any sweet talking. You're the law around here and you've been injured. I can't rightly kick you out."

Walt cleared his throat. "Technically, *I'm* the law around here, but I hear you."

"Thanks," Jonas mumbled.

Walt didn't acknowledge the comment. Instead, he put a hand on Eckert's arm and guided him out of the cubicle. "Let's make some calls and see if we can work through this."

"I'll just close this." With a nod, the nurse whipped the curtain around, providing them with a private cocoon.

Relief washed through Courtney the second Eckert left the room. She hadn't realized she was clenching the sheet in her hands. Her nails dug into her palms through the material.

"Rich, you stay for a second," Jonas called out when the other man stood up.

"Yes, sir."

Rich's smile eased away the rest of her anxiety. His body consisted of more bulk than Jonas's, and tension didn't tighten his face like it had with Jonas almost every moment she'd known him. "Is Jonas really your boss?"

"For now." Rich winked, but his relaxed stance disappeared when he got another look at Jonas. "Interesting day off you're having."

"Yeah, tell me about it." He plowed his fingers through his hair but swore when his arm got even with his chest.

Guilt pummeled her from every direction. She didn't like his chosen profession, but he'd killed for her, gotten injured for her. That meant something. "Are you okay?"

He nodded but his back teeth slammed together. "This is your last chance, Courtney. I need the truth. Do you know this Allen? Have you ever gone by the name Taynor?"

She settled for more half-truths. "No."

Jonas stared at her for a few beats. Much more and she'd be squirming on the mattress.

He finally turned back to Rich. "Okay, you go do some investigating. I want anything you can find on Eckert, Margaret Taynor and Peter Allen. Check Maryland, since that's where the original request came from. Someone started this by asking for the wellness check on this Taynor woman. Dig back through people until you find out who asked and why he thinks he's married to Courtney."

Rich's gaze skipped to her then back to Jonas. "What will you be doing while I work?"

"Getting Courtney out of here."

Finally. She exhaled the breath she'd been holding. It ripped from her lungs with a whoosh. Danger still lingered, but the crushing weight lifted. She needed her freedom. She couldn't investigate the murders while fighting off a trumped-up claim. Worse, she couldn't handle being dragged back to Maryland and shoved right into the path of someone who might want the last of the Peters family dead.

She went through her prepared mental list for her exit plan. "I just need a rental car."

Jonas shook his head. "Wrong. You're coming with me and staying with me until I understand what's happening."

She waited for the usual dread and claustrophobia to overwhelm her but it didn't come. Something about having a man on her side who owned a gun and knew how to use it felt right this time. Sure, he didn't believe her and had no idea the depth of the mess he was wading into, but he radiated strength and self-assurance, and she needed both right now.

But being smart enough to grab on to help didn't mean she would just roll over to his bossiness. "Do I get a say in what happens to me?"

"No." Jonas stepped closer to the opening of the cubicle and looked out. "Rich, try to keep Walt and Eckert at the entrance to the emergency room. I'll sneak her out through the door a few cubicles down. It leads into the main hospital. We can get to the lobby from there."

Rich nodded in her direction. "She's still hooked up to machines."

"I can take care of that." She tugged on the needle in her arm. The flash of pain stole her breath. "Whoa, that hurt like a—"

Rich cleared his throat as he turned his back to her and moved in closer to Jonas's side. "Are you, uh, sure you—"

"I'm fine and Courtney isn't going to kill me. She had the opportunity to shoot me and didn't. Besides that, I think she's figured out I'm the best chance she has for getting through this." Jonas looked over his shoulder at her. "Right?"

"She's hoping that's not true," she said in her clearest you're-annoying-me tone.

Jonas shrugged. "See? She's fine."

"Where are we going, exactly?" she asked before he could say something else to annoy her.

"I'll figure that out as we go." He stalked back to the bed and folded down the sheet. "Ready?"

Good thing she still wore her clothes. Grimy and sticky, she was desperate to shower and change, but that hadn't happened yet. "No."

"That's the spirit."

Chapter Six

Jonas pushed Courtney in a wheelchair. It and a change of clothes for both of them appeared right after Nurse Ramsey walked by the cubicle. The woman might be ornery, but she was also helpful.

With the cover, they made it to the side door. Without it who knew how bad the ride might have been.

Jonas stopped at the keypad next to the hospital entrance. The emergency security code for law-enforcement personnel popped into his head. Until his fingers touched the pad he wasn't sure he'd remember the needed sequence.

He pushed Courtney down the long hallway lined with beige tiles on the floor and matching beige paint on the walls. The general blahness of the place escaped him in previous visits. He'd been too busy worrying about securing the people with him and blocking out the harsh ammonia smell to notice.

"I can walk," Courtney said from the seat.

"The goal is to blend in and get you out of here without being seen." Then he had to keep her alive and figure out who was trying to do the opposite.

Yeah, no problem there.

The woman had secrets. He understood that. Accepted it. His years in the Los Angeles Division of the Drug Enforcement Agency working in narcotics trafficking taught him about human nature. His heart hardened, and his warning shots now came faster. Whatever she'd seen had the same effect on her.

"Were medical scrubs and a towel over my head the only options?" she asked.

Last thing he wanted to do was think about her clothing or her getting dressed or anything in between. Turning his back while she changed in the cramped cubicle nearly killed his control. "You're welcome."

"I meant that I could run faster in something else. I didn't mean to sound ungrateful," she said, sounding slightly more grateful than she had the second before.

"Really? It's sort of hard to tell with you sometimes."

She sighed loud enough for him to hear it over the clang of machines and low hum of televisions coming through the open doors of the rooms. "Now what?"

"We get out of here, head back to Aberdeen and go to your house."

"Won't the bad guys know to look there?"

"I hope so, but I doubt I'm that lucky." No, this whole sordid scene wasn't over yet. He might not be the smartest guy in the world, but he knew that much.

She grabbed the wheel and slammed their progress to a stop. As she spun around to face him, fire lit her eyes. "Maybe you need to rethink this plan. I'm not really in favor of one where we get chased again."

"Understood, but we can get some things for you. And since you don't like your current outfit…" He let the words sit there as a not-so-gentle reminder.

She waved her hand in front of her face. "Forget what I said. The clothes are fine. I don't need anything else."

He took in the rise of her chin and the way she rubbed her hands together until they glowed red. The tough-chick act hid something deeper. He knew she was under fire now. He wondered if she'd always been in that position.

"How long have you been running from the law?" he asked.

"I've never run from the law. Done a few laps to escape my past, but that's it."

She never broke eye contact. Either she could lie and not even twitch in reaction, or the trouble that followed her was not of her own making.

He wanted to believe the latter, but history had delivered the painful lesson that the former was often true. Psychopaths crawled around in every walk of life, including bosses and possibly women who went by the name Courtney.

"Ready to tell me about your past?" he asked.

Her eyebrow lifted. "Is now the time?"

"I might need—" He glanced down the hallway and saw a flash of a black suit before it disappeared around the corner. "Damn."

"What?"

Jonas would recognize the cocky walk and perfect posture anywhere. "Eckert."

"Where?"

"Up ahead. Slouch down."

She did it without saying a word.

Nice and smooth to avoid drawing attention, Jonas pulled the wheelchair backward. With his elbow against the door behind him, he pushed it open and swept Courtney inside.

"How did he know to come looking for us over here?" Her whispered question echoed in the quiet room.

The man in the bed didn't move. His white hair stuck out from beneath a pile of covers despite the heater running full force. From the outline of his body, Jonas pegged the guy as old and frail.

Getting out of there fast and without bloodshed was the

priority. The poor guy could have a heart attack if he woke up to strangers in his room. And if the bullets flew, they'd all have to dodge them.

"Bigger question is how Eckert gave two experienced law-enforcement officers the slip back in the emergency room. Rich and Walt should have been right there with him." Jonas pushed out the worry for his friends' safety. They could fight off Eckert, and the man wasn't likely to open fire in the hospital unless he had Courtney in his arms and could get out fast.

Jonas wasn't about to let her go. She pressed against his side as he peered out the crack in the closed door. He hadn't heard her move. The light touch impressed him.

"We have to sneak out," he said.

"Is Eckert really FBI?"

She gave voice to Jonas's worries as he thought them. A legitimate agent would play by the rules. There were smart ways for federal agents to walk into town and ask for help, usual channels. This guy ignored them all.

"If he is, this trip is off the books."

She wound her fingers into the scrubs he wore to cover his bare chest. "So, another assassin."

"Let's not use that word." Managing her panic took a top slot to getting her out of there. If she went wild, Jonas would have to knock her out, and the idea of hitting her gave him a nasty taste in his mouth. "There's an emergency exit at the opposite end of the hall."

"The same side where you just saw Eckert?"

"Unfortunately, yes. But Eckert kept moving. He's probably walking up and down the halls, which could give us the few seconds we need."

"I don't love this plan. How about doubling back into the emergency room, since we know he's not in there?"

"We're locked out on this side and I don't want to take the

time to stop and fumble with the code." Jonas grabbed her hand, letting the warmth of his body soak into her icy fingers. "We walk down the hall. When you get to the door, run fast and don't stop. No matter what, you leave the hospital."

"Without you?"

"If you have to." She looked a bit too happy at the thought for his liking. "Ready?"

She nodded. "Walk, sprint and keep going. Got it."

He didn't wait for her to think about it, turn it over in her head and obsess. "Now."

They slipped out of the room and walked double time to the end of the hall. They'd almost gotten to the spot where the hallways intersected when Eckert stepped out next to a cart stacked with supplies. He stood right in front of the door, his back to it, blocking it.

"I had a feeling you were in this hallway," he said.

Jonas squeezed her hand. "Go."

She took off.

When Eckert pivoted to catch her in midrun, Jonas dived. The shot hit Eckert right in the stomach, pushing him sideways and sending his full weight slamming into the wall behind him with a grunt. Jonas's shoulder screamed in protest. The second their bodies clashed, his arm caught on fire. His fingers tingled and daggers of pain sliced through his arm.

A cart crashed to the ground and metal pinged as pans fell to the tile floor. Jonas could hear the rush of footsteps around them and hear the shouts for them to stop. All that mattered was Courtney's successful flight to freedom. He blocked out the crowd noise and the scratching of hands against his arms and shoulders as a few bystanders tried to pull them apart.

Jonas refused to back away. He threw his weight into the man's stomach a second time.

Eckert's lean frame bent over, but he didn't go down.

Grabbing Jonas's shirt, Eckert pulled and punched. His fists landed with hard slams against Jonas's bruised ribs. It was as if the guy knew where to hit to inflict the most damage. He was no novice.

Jonas dropped to his knees as new shots of pain raced through him. The guy turned, trying to drag Jonas behind him to the door and flick him off like unwanted gum on his shoe. Jonas tightened his hold. His fist aimed for the back of Eckert's knee then his thigh. With a roar, the other man stumbled, sending them both flying back into the wall again.

Jonas scrambled from his knees and hit Eckert in the chest this time. The air coughed out of the man's lungs as he doubled over. Hunched over and wheezing, they circled each other. Every inch of Jonas's body ached and cried out for rest. He pushed it all out to focus on the snarling man across from him.

Ready to go again, Jonas shifted his weight to aim another hit. A flash of green streaked over Eckert's shoulder. The unexpected color took him off his game, shook his concentration. Eckert landed a solid punch to the jaw that sent Jonas's head bouncing back.

He blinked out the darkness. When his vision returned he saw Courtney's arms shake as she held a box the size of a toaster oven with dials on it and cords hanging down from the back, a piece of equipment of some type.

Eckert's eyes grew wide as if he sensed danger behind him. He turned just in time for her to lift the dark square over her head and crash it down on the side of Eckert's skull. He went boneless. His body slumped to the floor as blood trickled from his temple.

People crowded in from every direction. Many were shouting. Two men held on to Jonas's arms. He fought through it all, the chaos and the disbelief. Someone shouted something about calling the police.

Courtney muscled her way into the crowd and shoved everyone else aside. "He *is* the police."

In the stunned mumbling and rapid-fire questions that followed, she maneuvered him to the stairs. He called out over his shoulder to a nurse hovering over Eckert. "Page the sheriff. Walt Roberts. He's in the building."

Then they were out the door and the cool air hit Jonas's face, reviving his tired muscles. He'd taken ten steps before his brain jump-started again. "I told you to run and not look back."

She looped her arm through his. "I had to save you first."

He hated to admit it, but leaning against her was the only thing keeping him on his feet. "I should say thank-you."

"You can do that if we somehow get through this."

Chapter Seven

Kurt boarded the private plane late that afternoon. The crew had been on standby all day, with the manifest ready and his bags packed.

As the hours ticked by, dread washed over Kurt. He canceled meetings and put off phone calls. His private line rang three times, none with the news he wanted to hear.

Making the trip was the right thing to do. He invented a business problem and sent the wife to a spa. The kids had their own lives now and didn't need him. He could devote all of his attention to handling this problem before it exploded into a full-blown disaster.

He slid into the soft leather seat and dumped his briefcase on the table. Sitting back, he helped himself to a glass of scotch and let his mind go blank. The smell of jet fuel burned through his nose and the roar of the engine blocked his ears. For a few seconds he enjoyed the peace that came from watching others work as the pilots conducted their last-minute checks.

He'd be busy from the second he touched down in Oregon.

And when he returned it would all be over. Finally.

INSTEAD OF GOING to the hospital lobby and out into the fresh air, Jonas steered them down another flight to the basement.

A few flashes of his badge later and they stood in a window-less office lined with television monitors.

Courtney wished she had the kind of power to send people scurrying to help her. That had never been her life. She'd begged and no one listened. Having the reputation of "the woman who refused to believe" didn't open any doors for her.

"Here you go, sir." The man in the brown uniform and a tag that read Security clicked a few keys, and the dark screen on the far right flickered to life. "Just use these buttons to rewind and fast-forward."

Jonas's fingers hovered over the keyboard. "I'll need to confiscate the video."

"Sheriff Roberts already called about getting the daily security disc." The guard pointed to a red button. "Push this and it will eject. A backup disc is running and will take over."

"Good, because we'll need to keep taping for as long as this patient—" Jonas tapped another monitor showing Eckert being loaded onto a stretcher "—is here."

"Do you want me to get the sheriff now so you guys can work out jurisdiction or whatever?"

She waited for Jonas to throw his weight around or start issuing orders. In her experience, the guy with the highest rank and biggest mouth took over, regardless of his competency for the task.

"No," Jonas said, his voice filled with calm detachment. "Walt's busy handling the problem upstairs."

The guard finally looked at her. "Nice shot to that guy's head with the equipment, by the way."

She had no idea what to say, so she smiled back. She waited until the man left before studying the images on the screens. "I thought we were leaving."

"Soon."

She pulled up a chair and sat down next to Jonas. The urge to press her hand to his cheek nearly swamped her, but she fought it back. "Honestly, you don't look too good."

"Thanks."

He'd been through an accident and a fight. From the messed-up hair, the blood soaking through his bandage and the new bruises around his jaw, he looked more as if he'd been thrown under a car than tossed around in one.

And every cut and ache traced back to her. The least she could do was make sure he stayed on his feet long enough to get some help. "I'm thinking you need medical attention."

"We're in the right place."

"A small room in the basement?"

"At least it's at the bottom of a hospital."

The man needed a keeper. "Jonas, I'm serious here."

"I want to take a quick look at this security tape." He hit Rewind, and the scene with Eckert flew by.

"There." She got a glimpse of her image on-screen and thought she didn't look so hot, either.

"Let's see what we have."

The sight of them walking backward in double time mesmerized her. "Why is it important?"

"I want to see how Eckert got free and what he was doing while he roamed around the hospital."

They could look later, but she knew she'd never convince Jonas of that. On a mission, he sat there, focused, while he winced with even small movements of his arm.

"Stop." She pointed at the screen. "There he is."

Eckert stood huddled in a hallway corner. After glancing around, he turned and took something out of his pocket.

Jonas tapped the button so they could watch the scene frame by frame. "He's talking on a phone."

"Does that mean something to you?"

"He's in the middle of tracking you down and takes the

time to make a call?" Jonas swore. "I'm thinking it means he's reporting back to someone else."

When Jonas put it like that, she got it. The call meant a coordinated effort to track her. The guy in the forest, this one at the hospital. This had gone past checking up on her activities. Someone wanted to take her out and was employing a group of people to make it happen.

The chill inside her turned to a frantic shake. She had to concentrate to keep her teeth from rattling. "If you're trying to scare me, it's working."

Jonas gave her a sideways glance. "I would have thought getting run down, threatened and chased would have done it."

"Maybe the adrenaline is running out."

"Then it's time to leave." He popped the disc out and stood up.

"I guess you're still insisting I stay with you."

"Would you honestly prefer to go it alone?" He held out a hand.

She took it and let him help her to her feet. After all, he wasn't the only one who had been banged up and needed a break from the attacks. "No."

"Happy we've heard the last of that argument."

"I know I didn't say that."

Walt stuck his head in the room. "Jonas?"

"Hey." Jonas dropped her hand. "How's Eckert?"

"Out cold."

The need to defend her actions rose up and oozed through every part of her. "I didn't have much of a choice. He went after Jonas."

Walt raised an eyebrow. "So you hit the guy with an EKG machine."

"It was handy." Her skin tingled when Jonas spread a hand over her lower back with each finger pressing into her.

"She's resourceful," he said.

Walt's gaze scanned the monitors and counters. "What are you doing in here?"

"Grabbing the tape." Jonas held up the disc between two fingers.

"I would have gotten it."

Jonas palmed the disc and slipped it in his back pocket. "Sure, but I wanted to check it out."

Courtney listened to the staccato conversation. Walt acted the role of father and Jonas fought the interference with every step. With his stubbornness, she'd put money on Jonas winning the battle. It wasn't a matter of youth. It had to do with determination. The man was all grit.

"Maybe you should take the rest of the day off. Let me check everything and report back." Walt leaned against the door frame. "You guys have been through it, especially Jonas. Did the doctor clear you on the concussion?"

"I'll be fine."

"Never thought you couldn't handle the job. That's not my point here." Walt smiled at her. "Can I take you somewhere, Ms. Allen?"

No way was she stepping into the middle of this testosterone contest. She'd already picked a side. "I'm going with Jonas."

"Fine by me." Jonas gave a gentle push to lead them to the door. "We'll be at my office. Perfectly safe."

"I'll have my guy drive you." Walt reached for his radio.

"Much appreciated." Jonas nodded. "Before we head out, can you give me the rundown on the rest?"

"I have it under control. Eckert will be here overnight and I'll have a man on his door. Rich is doing some background research." Walt cleared his throat. "I asked him to do an extensive search on all angles then fill us both in."

"Thanks," Jonas said.

Walt hesitated, his gaze jumping between Jonas and Courtney. "I'll let my guy know you're ready to go."

She watched the older man leave and smiled at Jonas's cluelessness. Once they were alone she elbowed him. "He meant Rich is checking up on me."

"Yeah, I got that from the angles part." Jonas's sudden stop made her miss a step.

"What are you—"

He put a hand across the door and blocked the exit before she could step out. "Tell me something. What exactly will Rich find out about you? During all that digging?"

She knew Jonas expected the discovery of reams of paper that would explain every little detail of her life. He probably figured he'd get the pieces and work them until they fit together and made sense.

But life didn't work that way. Not hers, anyway. Nothing came easy, and words in a report couldn't begin to capture the reality.

"If I tell you, you'll spend the rest of the day interrogating me instead of resting." As soon as the words left her mouth the last of her energy expired and exhaustion hit. The double attack threatened to drop her to her knees. "And, honestly, I have to lie down because my brain is jumbled."

"You can't leave the conversation there." The corner of his mouth lifted. "Give me one hint and I promise not to ask you anything more today. I'll let it drop."

The silence stretched for almost a minute. She counted out the dragging seconds, weighing the pros and cons of taking the step she'd avoided for years. Once she did, running wouldn't be an option. No way would Jonas hesitate long enough for her to escape.

He lowered his head until he had eye contact again. "Courtney?"

She exhaled every doubt. "You'll find out I didn't exist until ten years ago."

His smile vanished. "What?"

"I think you heard me."

He straightened up. "But—"

"You promised."

He swore under his breath. "I'm sorry I made the deal."

"In fairness, I tried to warn you."

Chapter Eight

The next day Cade Willis sat in his rental car and stared across the street at the front door of a Craftsman bungalow. He'd come three thousand miles and taken almost ten years to get here.

Houses lined the quiet street, packed together with little room between them. He lived in a condo. Spent hours in a box with a row of windows on one side, only to leave and work in a bigger box.

But he wasn't on duty now. It was just after nine in the morning. He'd flown from Virginia to Oregon for one reason, and his first attempt to get to her had failed. Cade didn't know anything about Jonas Porter, but he would investigate. That was what he did. Researched, asked questions, studied the pieces and found answers. He'd been trained, but this was personal.

A woman, a little too old to be the *right* woman, blonde and curvy, walked up to the porch and used a key to open the front door. He glanced down to double-check the age-progressed photo in the file on the passenger seat. He flipped to the grainy one his investigator had taken last week.

He glanced up in time to see the unknown woman disappear inside the house. A long skirt and a sweater, short hair and a larger build. Yeah, definitely not the right woman.

He'd gathered hundreds of details about the woman he'd

been tracking, many of which came from his memory. He'd been fifteen the first time he saw her and twenty the last time they lived in the same place. The years since passed with terrible slowness. That was what happened when you lived under a cloud, when people judged you and pointed.

In the years since it all fell apart, he'd pushed and struggled. He'd done everything to turn his life around, but the past ran just a foot or two behind him, waiting to lunge and tackle.

He tempered every commendation with the knowledge unfinished business lurked. He knew from experience hard work wasn't always enough. Everything a man earned and accumulated, from his good name to the food in the refrigerator, could be taken away in an instant.

The person who threatened to do that to him had changed her name. Ann Peters faded away, leaving nothing behind to signal her existence except a series of newspaper articles and a few links at conspiracy-theory sites on the internet. She didn't exist. Her social security number lay dormant. No bank accounts or credit cards. No paper trail at all.

He'd wanted confirmation. Needed to see if wild child Ann Courtney Peters had morphed into respected illustrator Courtney Allen. He admired reinvention, but he refused to live in the past alone.

She started this.

He would finish it.

JONAS PARKED THE POLICE CAR in the alley behind her street, just two houses down from hers. After a night of her sleeping on his office couch while he slept in the desk chair, he winced every time he moved. He'd actually hissed when he reached around to put on his seat belt after leaving the office.

Through it all, he'd kept his part of the deal and hadn't asked a single question about her past. Didn't even sneak onto the computer, though Courtney would bet what little cash she had on her that he'd wanted to.

Now he stared ahead, watching the drizzle from the sudden storm hit the windshield as he tapped his fingers against the steering wheel. She didn't know what song played in his head because the inside of the car stayed silent except for the rhythmic swish of the wipers.

The quiet finally broke her. "Are we just going to sit here?"

Her insides jumped around, and she'd bargain with the devil for a shower at this point. Splashing in his office bathroom hadn't done the trick.

Jonas's frown deepened. "I think there's someone in your house."

"What?" She leaned down, trying to get a clear view of her back door from the passenger side of the car. "How can you know that?"

"I saw a shadow."

She glanced at him to make sure he wasn't joking. The severe frown suggested not. "How can you see anything from this far away?"

He looked at her then. "You can't?"

This qualified as one of the many conversations she'd wanted to avoid. Not that she spent hours worrying about her looks, because she didn't, but her eye issues were a constant source of annoyance. She could sit bent over her drawing table for hours, not even twitch when her lower back cramped up and begged for mercy, but when her vision blurred she stopped. Eyestrain quickly switched to double vision, which led to balance issues.

She'd suffered from the problem since she was a kid. There was a fancy name for it that she'd long forgotten and a chance the condition could worsen. It ruled out airplane pilot and a few other career choices. Drawing likely should have been one of them, but she'd refused to give it up.

A child's doodles became a source to release the pain of early adulthood and eventually her lifelong job. Illustrating books constituted nothing less than a passion now. The fact her love also paid the bills just made her one of those lucky people whose calling intersected with their career.

Unlucky in everything else, lucky in this—and she had no intention of throwing that away over a set of bum eyes.

She settled on telling Jonas the super-abbreviated version. "I wear glasses."

"Since when?" He acted as if they'd known each other for years and she hid a big secret.

"Always. I wasn't wearing my contacts when you arrived and had taken off my glasses to get the door, otherwise you'd know."

"Why didn't you wear the glasses to answer?"

That was not exactly the piece of information she thought he'd grab on to. "Just because."

Through the bandage over his eye and the cut near his mouth, he smiled. "Just so you know, the whole 'boys don't make passes at girls who wear glasses' thing is a lie."

"Oh, right. You find women in glasses sexy, I guess."

"Sure do."

"Are you messing with me?"

"Not yet."

Her stomach somersaulted. "Jonas—"

That quick, his attention switched back to the house. "Does anyone else have a key to your place? Friend, family member, boyfriend?"

The guy threw her off balance every time he opened his mouth. "Don't have either of the last two and very few of the first."

"You don't like people?"

"I like my privacy."

"Understandable." He opened his door. "I want you to stay here."

"No."

"Did you just say no?"

She took off the seat belt and cracked the door open before he could throw the parental safety locks. "I know you like issuing orders, but I'm done with feeling guilty about putting you in danger."

"You did see the badge, right? This is my job."

"I'm serious." Before he could argue, she got out of the car and started walking toward her backyard.

From the start, she'd intended to fight this battle alone. If he insisted on tagging along, fine, but she'd ensure he wasn't the primary target. She didn't have a death wish, but she did have experience with naive hope and empty promises, with incompetent cops and bad lawyers. Jonas didn't appear to fit in any of those categories but she wasn't ready to take a chance on that yet.

She'd stood at the gravesides of her mother and two sisters and made a vow. She was determined to keep it, no matter the consequences.

He stopped her with the press of his hand against her elbow. "Hold up."

She turned around, fire burning inside her, and let out a long, exaggerated breath. "You can't win this argument."

"Yeah, I get that. You're consistent."

"What does that mean?"

"You're not exactly a listen-to-the-rules type." He slipped a cell phone out of his back pocket with his good hand. "So, let's skip the part where you ignore me."

"Works for me."

"I'll go in and you stand in the alley. If I don't come out or you hear anything, you call Rich and get in that car."

"You're very big on going in alone."

"It's my job."

People once accused her of living on the blurred edge of safety. She looked at Jonas, with his injuries and clenched jaw of determination, and saw the danger simmering there. "I wonder."

"Don't dissect me." He flipped her hand over and dropped the phone in her palm.

When he closed his fingers over hers, the area around her heart trembled. "Fine, but don't be a hero. Just call for backup."

She'd never invited the police into her life before, but this was about Jonas. His safety, making sure he kept his distance from her mess.

"I can handle a house search on my own. Besides that, I have limited resources and personnel, and my people are busy taking turns watching the hospital and investigating." He squeezed her hand then let go. "Let's move."

Courtney didn't argue. She unlocked the gate at the back of the property. Quietly and with quick steps, they slid along the side fence with Jonas in the lead. When they reached the back door, he slipped her key into the lock, careful not to make a sound. He held up his hand and gave her the do-not-move glare.

As soon as his back disappeared into the house, she followed, catching the door before it banged against the jamb. She'd memorized every inch of the house and knew where to step and where someone could hide. He needed her.

He took two steps and stopped. His back straightened but he didn't turn around. "I thought I told you to wait this one out."

"And I thought I made it clear I was done being ordered around," she said in a low hush, mimicking him.

With one arm, he scooped her behind him. The other hand held the gun. "Stay right there and keep that phone ready."

Her head pressed against his back as they shuffled through the white kitchen she loved so much. The plates with the little daisy in the center, the ones she'd found at an estate sale and stacked in the cabinets. The small pots of herbs lined up on the windowsill. She handpicked every piece as she built her first real home as an adult.

"You okay?" he asked in a rough whisper.

"Yeah."

She rested one hand in the deep groove between his shoulder blades. As she expected, not an ounce of fat on the guy. Trim waist and sleek muscles, a hard back and shiny hair. The warmth of his body and scent of the outdoors washed over her in a mix that was pure male. She felt him inhale.

"Damn."

She grabbed his biceps and peeked around him as he hit the doorway into the small dining room. "What?"

"Call Rich."

She pushed around Jonas and stood by his side. The drawers to her sideboard stood open. Looking through to the family room, paperwork spilled out of her desk and couch cushions lay scattered on the floor.

She tried to push past him. "My house."

"Hold on." He pressed a hand to her stomach. "Wait here."

The guy just wasn't getting it. She's sat on the sidelines, passive and still, and watched her life spin. Those days were officially over. She was about to argue with him while she hit the button for Rich's line when the hardwood floor creaked near the front door. She kept it loose on purpose. It was her first line of defense. Looked as if the system worked.

His gaze shot to hers. He mouthed the word *company* and nodded toward the back door. This time she listened. Coming face-to-face with another gun didn't interest her.

With lightning speed, he whipped into the family room, gun up and shoes quiet against the usually creaky floor. "Stop! Police!"

The high-pitched scream and heavy thud had Courtney running into the room after him. She told Rich to hold as her gaze went to the front door. Jonas had someone pinned against the wood as he reached around for his handcuffs.

Sneakers, flowing skirt, yelling. The woman bucked and slammed her body against his as she tried to land a kick. "Get off of me!"

Instant recognition.

"Jonas, no." Courtney reached them just in time to grab his wrist. The handcuffs jangled in his fingers. "She's not a thief."

Confusion fell over his face. "Who is it?"

"You're the deputy."

"That doesn't mean I know everyone."

When her friend started wiggling and mumbling, Courtney rushed to end the wrestling without more trouble. "That's Ellie."

He didn't let up on the elbow pressed into Ellie's back. "Be more specific."

Courtney tugged on his arm to get him to back up. "Ellie Wise, best friend and landlord."

Jonas loosened his hold then held his hands up as if waiting to get that kick he'd been fighting off. "I see."

Ellie turned around. Fury blazed in her chocolate-brown eyes. "That's all you have to say?"

"How about this…how did you get in here?"

Ellie held out her hand. "My key."

Courtney felt the rush of guilt down to her toes. "I forgot she had one."

"What's going on?" Ellie looked at them, then around the house. "I heard you were in the hospital and came to get some stuff for you. There's stuff everywhere. The bedrooms look even worse. You've got this one on guard."

Stuff everywhere. Panic rose in her throat. Courtney spun around and raced to the fireplace on the far wall.

Dropping to her knees, she ignored the pain assaulting her and stuck her hand up the fireplace, digging around in the ashes. Her fingers touched on the corner and she tugged. Her shoulders slumped in relief as she pulled the folder out of its hiding place and sat back on her knees with it clutched to her chest.

By the time she looked up, both Ellie and Jonas hovered over her with matching frowns.

"What are you doing?" Jonas asked.

Courtney hugged the envelope and rocked. "He didn't find it."

Ellie shook her head. "What are you talking about?"

"Who?" Jonas asked at the same time.

Courtney decided to answer them both at the same time. "The man who murdered my family then framed my dad for it."

Chapter Nine

Cade walked down the hospital hallway toward room two-fifteen. He didn't look at the numbers as he passed. Didn't need to. The guard standing watch in front of the door at the end of the hall guided the way.

Cade stopped in front of a young officer. The guy looked all of twenty, even with the military haircut and gun within inches of his hand. The name tag said Stimpson. The flat line of his mouth said business.

Stimpson held up one hand while the other went to the top of his weapon. "This is a restricted area."

"I'm here to see Paul Eckert."

"No one goes in or out. Deputy Porter's orders."

Jonas Porter again. The guy caused trouble without even being there. "I have something that trumps your deputy."

Stimpson snorted. "I doubt that."

The challenge intrigued Cade. He held his shiny badge, ready to go, and flipped it open. "FBI. Now, step aside."

Stimpson's scowl faltered. "I was told—"

"Call your deputy. In the meantime, I'm going in that room." This time when Cade stepped forward, Stimpson shifted to the side.

But he caught the door before Cade could shut it. "This stays open until I get confirmation."

Good for Stimpson. "Agreed."

Cade took it all in—the heart-rate monitor, the bandage on Paul's head and around his hand. Dressed in a hospital gown with the covers pulled up to his chest, he looked less like the ace Academy grad who now specialized in white-collar crime and more like an actual patient.

"You owe me." Paul's eyes opened the second after he made his comment.

"You heard my talk with Stimpson?"

"Way I figure it, you have about five minutes before that Porter guy comes rushing through the door."

"I'll be out in four." Cade nodded in the direction of the beeping monitor. "You okay?"

"Waiting for the scan to come back, but the brain appears to be working. Ducking police questions has been tougher. They're persistent out here." Paul lowered his voice. "Man, what did you get me into? You know they're calling the office and checking my credentials?"

Cade regretted getting his friend involved. Cade had called in a favor and made up a story. "Since you actually are an agent, you'll be fine."

"But we both know this isn't a real assignment."

Cade blocked out that part. He'd do everything he could to make sure Paul didn't get in trouble. The fake backstory was in place and ready to go. Signed documents and the right computer trail waited in case anyone went snooping.

But that left the bigger question. The one Cade could not kick out of his head. "You were supposed to talk with her, not get into a fight and land here."

"Thanks for caring about my future with the Bureau."

Cade put a hand on the back of the bed above Paul's pillow and leaned in. "I'll handle it."

And Cade could. He'd gone from newbie to supervisor in record time. Flew up the rigid promotion system and passed men with years more experience. That rapid rise gave him power. A few forms and rerouted calls, and everything would work out.

If Porter backed off, it would all go away immediately. Cade guessed he wasn't going to be that lucky.

Paul nodded but didn't look convinced. "When I saw her getting loaded into the ambulance, I wanted to make sure she was okay. Also figured I'd follow her here and make a move. Even had the help of the local sheriff."

"Porter?"

"He's town police. This is another guy. Walt something."

"And?"

"Porter tried to sneak her out of the hospital. I knew it was going to happen, sensed the guy had a personal stake in her, and held back. When he took her out, I followed to keep track for you and, well, hell, the guy saw me and went ballistic."

The more Cade heard about Porter, the harder Cade's headache hammered. So many years, so much planning. Having it ruined by a cop with a hard case of lust made Cade want to punch something.

"Tell me about Courtney Allen," Cade said.

"It's her. Different name but definitely a match to the woman you've been hunting."

Cade hadn't known he was holding his breath until it rushed out of him. "Good."

"But something else is going on."

Cade didn't move. There was no way Paul could know every detail. "Meaning?"

"She got into trouble out in the forest. Before that, I heard him at her front door, talking about some other woman."

Cade's world shifted back into place. Paul didn't know. He hadn't figured out every detail.

Paul snapped his fingers. "Maggie or Margaret. Something like that."

The headache thundered until Cade could barely hear anything else. "Taynor. The name is Margaret Taynor."

"That's it. The name sounds familiar, but I couldn't place it. Who is she?"

"A lawyer."

Paul held up his hands. "That narrows it down. We only know about ten thousand of them in D.C."

"A dead one."

All amusement left Paul's face. His anger highlighted the bruise around his eye. "Look, Cade. I said I'd take a few days off and help you out, play a part, so you could reel this witness in, but—"

"She's not a witness."

Paul's mouth dropped open. "You mean she's really wanted on something?"

"Yes."

"What the…" His bed whirred as he hit the button and struggled to sit up. "Why didn't you do this job by the rules? This isn't like you."

"We don't have time for explanations. Suffice to say I haven't told you everything, but I will."

"I don't like it. You're messing with my life here, Cade."

He glanced over his shoulder and saw the officer talking on the phone. "I'm going to see about getting you out of here and erasing any record of your time here except the official record, which I'll write."

"How are you going to get all of the people here to stay quiet? I've had law enforcement crawling all over me since I arrived."

"Let me worry about that. Your job is to get dressed. When the nurse comes in, I want you to be ready to go."

"To where?"

"Home, and don't talk to anyone. Keep with the same story. Flash the badge and refuse to comment on a pending investigation." Cade thought about the file in his car. "I'll handle Courtney from here."

SEEING COURTNEY FIGHT ALL DAY, watching the fear fall over her and her push it back, made Jonas view her in a certain way. Tough, determined, not afraid to break the rules.

He'd prepared his mind for a criminal past even as the rest of him rebelled at that thought. He expected talk about some minor crimes in her past that didn't matter. He preferred that to an ex who hurt her and had her on the run.

But the gem about her name being new threw him. Even with every ounce of energy drained from his broken body, he'd fidgeted in that chair for hours the night before thinking about what she didn't say.

Nothing readied him for news of a mass murder.

Standing next to her now, seeing the energy bounce off her as she gripped the folder as if it were the only thing holding her upright, showed him another side. Vulnerable. This wasn't about her refusing to own up to something. This was about her wading right into the middle of a disaster.

A dead body in the forest. A rogue FBI agent. And now a tossed house.

He could forget about sleep for at least another day. No way was he leaving her alone or with anyone else. Jonas trusted Walt and Rich with his life, but that didn't mean he could walk away.

Not from this. Not from her.

"When and where?" he asked.

Courtney's throat bobbled. "Maryland, ten years ago."

"I don't understand. Why didn't you ever say anything?" Ellie stood there with her feet rooted to the floor and her breaths coming in hard puffs.

Courtney shook her head. "I never talk about…"

"You don't want to relive it," he said.

"People called my dad a family annihilator, a guy who wipes out his wife and kids." She gulped in a huge breath. "I still can't believe it happens often enough for there to be a term for it."

Jonas knew all about the definition and the type of man who would commit such a heinous crime. On the outside, he appeared dedicated to his family but doubts and frustrations festered. Possessive, controlling and narcissistic. The idea of Courtney being a victim of such a man, even a dead one, made Jonas want to punch something.

Despite his rising anger over the situation, Jonas had to tread carefully. One wrong word and Courtney would get it into her head he didn't believe her and close down.

"Your father was found guilty?" Jonas knew with enough time and a little information he could find the answer, but he wanted to hear it from her. He sensed she needed to say it, to let some of the poison out.

Her fingers curled tighter on the folder. "He was found dead at the scene. Gunshot wound to the head."

"I'm so sorry." Ellie reached out a hand but stopped short of touching Courtney.

"Where were you when it happened?" Jonas asked, trying to stay all business so she could get the information out without crumbling, though she didn't strike him as the crumbling type.

Ellie put her body in front of her friend's. "What are you saying?"

He shifted until he faced Courtney head-on again. "Courtney?"

She didn't need sympathy now. Determination radiated off of her. What she needed, what he read from the tone of her voice and the sadness in her eyes, was to be heard.

He'd been trained to listen, no matter how painful the facts. Usually he had the small comfort of distance. He didn't know the victims and could build an emotional barrier. After only a few hours, he felt an attachment to Courtney. That would make everything harder.

"I'd snuck out to be with my boyfriend." The words sounded as if they were ripped out of her one by one.

The pieces shifted and fell together for Jonas. A young girl having fun and missing a massacre. Many would term it as fate, but he suspected there was something deeper going on—survivor's guilt.

"So, you lived," he said in the softest voice he could manage.

She never broke eye contact. "Yes."

Her answers brought more questions, but Jonas knew one thing for certain. He had to get her out of there. He didn't know how what was happening now was related to the killings then, but the invisible ties existed. He'd bet everything he had on it.

"It's time to move." He glanced around the room. "Gather everything you need—"

Courtney lifted the folder to just under her chin. "This is it."

"Wrong. Get some clothes and your glasses. Enough with the vanity. You need to see what's going on."

"What are you two talking about?" Ellie asked. Her gaze shifted between Courtney and Jonas.

"I'm taking her somewhere safe until I know who broke in here and why." A memory hit him. "If you each had to use a key to open a door, how did the person get in?"

Ellie hitched a thumb over her shoulder. "There's a window open in the bedroom."

"No." Courtney shook her head. "I never leave anything open or unlocked when I leave."

He knew that before she said it. Someone with her past

would guard her safety. "You'll pack a bag and come with me. We'll close up and Ellie will go home."

"How does any of that help Courtney?" Ellie asked.

"I'm going to be by her side until we figure this out."

Courtney's head tilted to the side as she shot him an unreadable expression. "And if you don't?"

"I will."

Chapter Ten

No one stood at the door. As promised, the guard had disappeared at the right moment.

With help from his inside contact, Kurt had disabled the security cameras. They had switched to a blank screen exactly one minute ago, allowing him time to slip in and out undetected.

He had the hospital pass clipped to his borrowed scrubs to help him blend. In the time it took to walk back and forth, he would wrap Cade Willis up in a tight knot that had him answering questions and fighting off murder allegations for months.

Like father, like son.

The best part: nothing would trace back to anyone other than Cade. An alibi, complete with video footage placing Kurt back in Washington, D.C., had been set up and readied. No record of him leaving the metro area existed. If anyone asked, he'd never been to Oregon.

But first, Kurt had to see if he could get any information out of Paul Eckert. Confirmation of his connection to Cade Willis would do. If the men were working together, Kurt still could close the loop. If the investigation had widened or become official, things could get messy.

Kurt eased open the door to room two-fifteen. The agent

wasn't in the bed, but the light in the bathroom burned in a thin line under the door.

Kurt loved when a plan came together. If only everything related to his dealings with Courtney had run this smoothly.

Putting on his black gloves, he moved to the bathroom. When the door opened, he shoved it back, slamming it into the agent's head. The man lifted his hands to his nose as he groaned. Kurt didn't wait. He pushed the agent against the sink and pressed the knife to his throat.

"Who are you working for?" Kurt asked.

The agent gasped as blood ran down his face. "Who the hell are you?"

"Wrong answer." The tip of the knife pricked skin. "Who?"

"I'm FBI. Agent Paul Eckert."

"I don't care." Kurt didn't have this kind of time. He'd been promised a few minutes alone and nothing more. As those ticked by, the chance of detection grew. And he could not allow that. "Are you in town on Cade Willis's orders or someone else's?"

The agent's confusion slipped for just a second before snapping back into place.

"I don't know who Cade Willis is. Never heard of him at all." Paul's voice sounded stronger, more sure.

He broke a very easy rule—using six words when one would do. The slip didn't get by Kurt. Sure, this guy played a role, trying not to give Cade away. Kurt admired the loyalty but didn't let it sidetrack him. Now that the agent regained his wits, puffing up his chest, making a move couldn't be far behind.

"You've been very helpful." Kurt sliced the knife deep into the agent's neck and stepped back.

Shock filled the man's dark eyes the second before he stumbled. His hands went to his throat as his fingers wrapped around the wound. He choked and gagged, trying to speak, but no words came out.

His body sagged against the sink as he threw a hand out for balance. Slick with the blood, he slipped and fell. His body bucked. He grabbed for Kurt's pants but missed.

Kurt took it all in. A dark blankness filled him as he watched the life drain out of the agent. He knew he should feel remorse, but this wasn't his fault. Courtney put this man in his path. Courtney refused to move on.

She caused this and she would be sorry.

COURTNEY SAT DOWN in the hard wooden chair across from Jonas's desk. She'd had her duffel bag and folder in hand, and they'd made it as far as his office again. He'd locked her precious cargo in the closet and promised to shoot anything that came in or out. Still, she stole a glance at the door every few minutes just to make sure.

She'd never been inside a police station willingly before. Her police phobia saw to that. Now she'd been in one twice in a few hours.

The one-story beige building stood in the middle of town, next to the mom-and-pop hardware store and across from the former movie theater currently being renovated to reopen as a restaurant. She knew about the new place because she'd been commissioned to design a graphic for the sign and the wall behind the bar.

She stared out the window at the construction truck in front of the building and let her mind wander. Jonas hadn't asked a single question about her family or her name change since they left her house. He sat behind his desk, and his fingers clicked away with impressive speed across his keyboard.

The silence wore her down. "You can say it, you know."

He didn't look up. "What?"

"Can we not pretend?" She'd spent so many years burying it. Maybe it was time to drag it into the light. "Please."

His fingers hovered over the keys. "You think I don't want to know every detail of what happened?"

"If you do you're hiding it well."

His gaze moved to hers. His body relaxed back into the chair cushion, but awareness shimmered off of him. "I was trying to be considerate of your feelings."

"Is that your usual style?"

He barked out a laugh. "No. I've become the rush-in type during recent years."

"What were you before?"

The smile left his face. "Too careful. Too willing to follow the rules even when I knew they were wrong."

The easy conversation calmed the spinning in her head. With each husky word he said, the tension seeped from her muscles. "That sounds like experience talking."

"Years working in Los Angeles, so I earned it the hard way."

"Want to tell me about it?"

"No."

"But I should spill, just tell you everything about my awful past?"

"I'm guessing we can only handle one personal history at a time."

"Any chance we can start with you?"

"Well." He sat forward, leaning on his elbows. "We could, but no one is trying to kill me."

"I find that hard to believe." After a stark beat of quiet, the rich sound of his laughter washed over her. Any last worries about being safe with him fled. "Admit it. You can be difficult."

"Bossy, demanding, controlling. Not the first time I've

heard any of those." He shrugged those wide shoulders. "I'd blame the job, but it's probably the personality type."

"I can think of a few other words to describe you."

His gaze roamed over her face. "Where are your glasses?"

"I put the contacts in." And her left eye had been watering ever since.

He made a tsk-tsk sound with his tongue. "Stubborn."

"You're right. I am. Feel free to gloat."

The smile left his face. "I'd rather hear the story."

Icy-cold fingers reached into her chest and grabbed her heart. She had no one else to blame. She'd opened a door and he'd jogged right through it. Sharing terrified her...until she stared into those eyes, the color of the cloudy sky right before a storm, and the powerful tug of unburdening hit her.

"It's taking every ounce of control I possess not to go online and search for myself. With a few calls, I'd likely have the official version," he said.

"Why didn't you?"

"I want to hear it from you." His expression remained unreadable as he laced his fingers together on top of his desk blotter. "I think maybe you need to say it."

The gate burst open before she could figure out a way to hold the words back. "Allen Peters."

"Your father, I'm guessing."

She nodded. "He was the type of guy who heard about a girl getting pregnant at the high school and grounded me to teach me a lesson."

Jonas's eyebrow lifted. "A tough guy."

She almost laughed at the understatement. "He could yell for hours, or so it seemed. Everything is exaggerated when you're a teenager, but I remember the house being loud." She hated how the laughter faded but the angry words remained.

"Where was your mother during all of this?"

"She would coax him into the bedroom and shut the door,

but the thick wood didn't blunt the sound. He'd spew and judge, curse and berate."

Jonas's eyes narrowed for a second before his blank stare returned. "That had to be hard to handle."

"He judged everyone and held us to a high standard."

"Maybe an unreasonable one?"

Being the only one sharing made her want to squirm right out of her chair. As it was, she had to sit on her hands to keep from fidgeting. "What was your dad like?"

"Tough but fair." Jonas launched right into a description, this time not evading the personal question. "A lifetime navy man. Mom died of breast cancer when I was in junior high, so it was just me and Dad."

She heard the pride laced through the minimum of words. Jonas didn't talk about the mutual love and respect because he didn't have to. She could see it. At the mention of his father, Jonas's face lit up, and the exhaustion that had been tugging at his mouth and eyes for the past hour disappeared.

He'd known loss but it didn't define him. Not like it did with her.

The kick of envy stole her breath. And his honest explanation kept her talking. "Mine came to my volleyball games and would shout and swear at the coaches from the stands."

Jonas nodded. "He was that guy."

"Totally."

"Abusive?"

Courtney turned the label over in her mind. It didn't fit. Nothing about her family, the situation, fell neatly into any category. "I never thought of him that way, but by most standards he'd be considered a jerk. He never hit but his words could knock you back."

How many times had she wondered if her parents would have made it had they lived? Too many to count. Not that the answer really mattered or solved the questions surrounding their murders, but for some reason the idea of their eventual divorce plagued her.

"That day I'd been grounded for a bad grade—a B, by the way—and ordered to come straight home. Furious and dramatic, in pure teen mode, I disobeyed. I didn't go home after school or call. I stayed with my boyfriend until past dark then went home, ready for a showdown."

She'd replayed that last week in her mind so many times. Her father spent almost every hour at home, locked in his office while he pored over paperwork. The man normally worked twelve-hour days at the office, going in before six so he would be home for the mandatory weekday family dinner, but that week he broke with his normal schedule.

"Courtney?" Jonas slipped a hand across the desk toward her. "We don't have to do this now."

She closed her eyes, grateful for his ticket out. The temptation proved great, but she forced her eyes open again. "I have to do it sometime. You need the information, right?"

"So I can help you, yes."

He was a man who wore every rough moment on his face. Handsome but not in a pretty way. Real, with scars and stubble and strength etched in every line. But when he looked at her just now the sharp angles of his face smoothed.

"The police officer met me in the driveway." Even with her eyes open and her life safe in a secure building, the flashing police lights twirled red and blue in her head. "My dad's business partner was there. Neighbors stood on the sidewalk, huddled together and whispering as I walked by."

"That's what neighbors do."

"No one approached me except the cop. He put his arm around my shoulders and told me everything would be fine. I had no idea who he was and I tried to listen, but the radio on his shoulder kept chirping." She tugged on the bottom of her ear. "Four dead. The refrain repeated until I couldn't hear anything else."

The night came back to her in a rush. The choking smell of exhaust from the fire truck by the curb. The police officers stretching yellow tape across her lawn. The front door standing open as people with blue windbreakers and small cases walked in and out.

"I remember thinking my dad would be pissed if he saw all of these people walking through the flower beds and going inside without taking off their shoes." She shook the remainder of the night out of her head and forced her mind to join her body back in today's world. "Weird, right?"

"Human. You remember him with a teenager's eye. That colors everything."

"I thought he'd called in all the police to scare me for staying out in violation of his orders."

Four dead.

"But when I didn't see my dad on the porch, I knew what the voice on the speaker meant." She forced the words up her throat. "Deb, Susie, Mom and Dad. All gone while I was kissing my boyfriend and giggling about how I was drinking a beer behind my dad's back."

She swallowed, unable to say anything. Closed her mind so the memories couldn't sneak back in.

Jonas flipped his hand over and let it lay palm up. "How old were you?"

With her finger she traced his from base to tip, each one turn after turn. Long and lean, strong and surprisingly soft. When she placed her hand in his, the warmth of his skin closed around her.

"Seventeen. One month from graduation."

When her eyes met his again she expected to see pity like she had with every social worker and lawyer, every cop and every teacher at school. While some people whispered behind her back wondering why she'd survived, others drowned her in sympathy. She preferred those bold enough to question why her dad would spare her—when he obviously preferred Susie—over those who wanted her to stay helpless and needy so they could save her and wash away the guilt of not seeing the tragedy before it happened.

The extended family split, her mother's relatives clamoring with stories about her dad's terrible behavior and her mother's desire to leave him. Her father's family sainted him. She got pulled and tugged from one end to the other until she walked away.

A name change and relocation later and she woke up without a past. Or she thought it would work that way.

"The police determined my father killed my mother in a moment of uncontrollable rage. That financial problems at work had piled up to push an already volatile man to the edge." She inhaled deep enough to flush her brain with a burst of fresh oxygen. "So he took out his family, thinking we were all home and that he could save us from the horrible life of poverty that lay ahead."

Jonas turned her hand over and slid it between both of his. "You lived."

"He didn't know I was gone."

Jonas lifted her hand to his mouth and pressed a soft kiss against her skin. "You don't believe the story."

It was about more than a belief. She knew down to those dark places in her soul that the police took a shortcut and got this one wrong. "Dad was imperfect but not a killer."

Jonas didn't debate or try to talk her out of it. "What's your theory?"

Her eyes searched his. So many people had asked the question then not listened to her answer. They wanted her to talk so they could analyze her or use her to close a case.

Not Jonas. He sat there, his attention focused on her and his hand wrapped around hers, and waited for her to speak.

She didn't have to come up with an elaborate scheme. She'd studied every angle. She had the entrances and exits mapped out and the details outlined. After begging the police to listen and offering theories no one would act on, she tucked the knowledge deep inside and vowed to step back into the light only after she had the evidence to end it all.

But sharing her findings proved easier with Jonas than she ever anticipated. He hit on the truth when he said she needed to tell. It was time and he was the right person.

"The landscape guy attacked my sister, Mom walked in and she was killed. The man then killed everyone, each as they came home, to hide his tracks."

"Do you know anything about the forensics—"

She dropped Jonas's hand and started to stand up. "I have it in my folder."

"Sit." The deputy part of him roared back to life.

"Jonas, I can prove it all to you."

"I believe you."

"I…" She had no idea what to say or how to handle the rumble of hope inside of her.

"We'll go through it." His gaze grew in intensity. "I will look at every document and test result. I'll call in every favor until I see all the information that exists on the case."

The rumble turned to a thundering wave. "You will?"

"I promise." He nodded back to the seat she just left and didn't continue until she dropped into it. "But right now I want you to tell me who you think is after you. This landscape guy? Is that like a gardener?"

"He's dead. Shot himself a few months after…they died. News stories circulated about his possible involvement and he put a gun in his mouth." And she hadn't spent one minute feeling sorry for the guy. No, she hated him for leaving before he could clear her father's name.

Jonas swore as he shook his head. "I'm not sure if that's ironic or just tragic."

"It's proof he couldn't take the guilt of what he'd done."

Jonas didn't say anything for a second. "So, you think the guy in the forest was financed by someone else? Couldn't be the gardener if he's out of the picture."

She knew exactly who sicced the attacker on her. They'd been circling each other for years. "His son. He's as desperate to clear his father's name as I am to clear mine."

"Sounds like a dangerous situation."

"It's a race to see who gets there first."

Chapter Eleven

Rich drank a cup of rancid hospital coffee as he pushed open the emergency-stairwell door to the second floor. Walt stepped off the elevator at the same time and they met in the middle.

Rich smiled over the rim. "It's only two floors, you know."

"When you're older you'll understand." Walt laughed as he tapped his rounded stomach.

"If you say so."

Walt cleared his throat. "How's Jonas?"

"I think you're asking if I think he's safe with Courtney."

"And?"

"She's a mystery. From what I can tell, she didn't even exist until a few years ago, and she's clearly on the run from her past, but I don't see a threat there."

Walt swore. "I think you're wrong. We need to do something before Jonas gets stuck on the wrong side of this thing."

"That will be tough, since Jonas doesn't want to be saved from her." Rich shook his head, his gaze catching the empty hallway in front of them. All amusement slammed to a halt. "Where's the guard?"

"What?"

With quick steps, Rich reached the nurses' station and dumped his drink on the counter. His gun came out a second later.

When a nurse gasped, he held up a hand to keep her quiet and still. "Keep everyone here."

Walt was a step behind him, radioing for assistance. "I need backup. Call security and get this hospital ready for lockdown on my signal."

"No one comes on or off this floor." Rich pointed at the elevator before turning back to Walt. "Where did your guy go?"

Without further discussion, both men took off at a run. Rich got to the room first and waited at the entrance for Walt to take his position on the opposite side of the door. With a nod, Rich took the lead. He shoved the door open with a shoulder, his gaze darting around the room.

He performed a mental checklist. Window closed. Room cleared. Bed empty.

Walt pointed to the red pool seeping from under the bathroom door. With a three count he opened it, and both men stared into Eckert's dead eyes.

JONAS ACHED FOR HER. Courtney lived a nightmare most people couldn't imagine. He'd taken victim statements and listened to the accused spew excuses and pretend innocence even as they drove a truck full of cocaine into a school playground. That hadn't prepared him to sit across from her and stay quiet while a horror film played in her head.

He'd seen stories on the news about family annihilators, but seeing her face as she relived the horror chipped away at something cold and frozen inside of him. The idea of subjecting her to more death tied a knot in his chest, but he didn't have a choice. Leaving her alone pushed his control to the breaking point.

He'd guided her with her head down to the back entrance to avoid the reporters gathering out front of the hospital. More than one person in the angry crowd gathered in the lobby tried to stop him and demanded answers, but he kept moving. Flashing his badge, he got them upstairs before anyone could get in the way.

"I have to be here." He delivered his lame explanation as they walked past the nurses huddled by the second-floor elevator and through the wall of uniformed officers blocking the entrance to the rest of the hallway.

"I know."

He stopped three doors away from the scene. "You can stay in the hall and—"

She broke his train of thought when she put her hand on his forearm. "I can handle it."

"From where I sit, you can do just about anything."

She gifted him with her first smile in hours. "That's good to know."

"We'll get to that later."

Right now he had to concentrate on death. The emergency call came in right as Courtney told her story. Rich insisted on breaking through and only needed one word to do it— Eckert.

Rich met them at the yellow tape cordoning off the last two rooms. He nodded to Courtney. "Ma'am."

Jonas shifted to business mode. "Give me the status."

"We've moved all the patients to other floors. Forensics is finishing up now, and Walt took care of the security cameras."

Jonas did a visual sweep of the long hall and U-shaped paths around the nurses' stations. People could hide right in the open here. "Any witnesses?"

"None. Even though it's early, the place is busy. Nurses aren't checking out every person to walk on the floor."

Jonas kept his back teeth locked tightly together to stop from yelling. If he started he wouldn't stop. "Where was our guard?"

"No idea. Walt's trying to find him now."

"His orders were clear." Jonas had issued them personally even though Walt's man stood at the door. "Do not move."

"He's missing?" Courtney asked.

Rich nodded. "Unfortunately, yes."

"Was Eckert really FBI?" she asked. With the rise in the rumble of voices from the door to the crime scene her gaze switched to the end of the hall.

A man backed out of the room with his hands on a gurney. The black zippered bag sat on top. The wheels creaked as it rolled by.

Her body went stiff. Jonas wished he could put an arm around her and usher her out of there.

Rich missed all the signs of distress and kept talking. "Eckert's story checked out insofar as he was here to question someone. When I asked about you and tried to dig into any pending cases linked to your name, I came up empty."

Her mouth dropped open. "I have no idea what that means."

In Jonas's mind it spelled trouble. More of it. "He was fishing. Looking for you. The question is why."

The FBI angle added a new dimension to the desperate and increasingly deadly situation. Fed involvement kicked up Jonas's heart rate and made him watch over his shoulder. In his experience, the guys who sat at the desks and didn't have a clue made the policies and put everyone at risk.

He'd walked away from his last job rather than get sucked into a never-ending cycle of bureaucratic interviews and forced mental-health checks. He'd followed the rules of engagement and a good man died. Now he didn't wait to shoot. He also didn't give automatic trust to everyone who carried a badge.

"Do you have access to the FBI database?" Courtney asked Rich.

He looked to Jonas then back to her again before answering. "I'm not sure what you're asking."

She bit her lower lip. "If I gave you a name, could you check and see if he has a work relationship with Eckert."

Jonas tried to follow her reasoning but couldn't see where she was going. "Who are you talking about?"

"Cade Willis." She didn't say anything else. Just stared at Jonas.

The answer smacked right into him. He didn't know how he knew, if the desperation in her eyes telegraphed the truth or something else clued him in. "The son?"

She nodded.

Rich held up a hand as if trying to get their attention. "I don't understand."

Jonas refused to violate her trust. Rich didn't need the details to dig. He could make the inquiries on a name. "Check it out without leaving fingerprints. I don't want this tracing back to us. Back channels only."

Rich didn't question or hesitate. "I'll start right now."

"Jonas?" Walt stepped out of the dead man's room and motioned for Jonas to join him.

When he turned back to Courtney she was already smiling. "Go. I won't move or touch anything."

"It's hard to believe twenty-four hours ago you tried to run from me."

Her eyes widened. "That was just yesterday?"

"I know how to show a woman a good time." He squeezed her elbow and ducked under the tape.

While Jonas glanced into the room, Walt stared at Courtney. "You brought a date to a crime scene?" he asked.

"This all centers on her."

"That's what has me concerned."

Jonas cut his visual inspection short. "Tell me what's ticking you off about her. Something has your distrust spiking."

Walt stepped farther into the room and pitched his voice low. "There is a lot of trouble following that woman. We now have two dead bodies. And as far as I can tell, the only connection is her."

"She's in danger."

Walt scratched his bald head. "Is she?"

"Clearly you have something to say. We've known each other long enough for you to just spit it out."

"What do you know about her?" he asked.

Despite the pull to defend her, Jonas refrained from making their time together bigger than it was. "I met her yesterday morning."

"And have been under fire ever since."

"I can handle it."

"The issue is whether it's time to cut her loose." When the forensic tech started taking photos of the room, Walt pulled Jonas closer to the window. "She's wanted by the FBI. Turn her over and be done."

"That's not true."

"What are you talking about?"

"Rich checked. There's no case. This—all of this, including my wellness visit—has been about locating her and getting close. And now the FBI agent with a supposed need to talk with her is dead."

"We had two homicides in five years until she came to town. That's what I'm focusing on at the moment."

Jonas refused to pile all that blame on Courtney and he wouldn't let anyone else do it, either. "She's been living here without trouble. This all came to her doorstep. She didn't ask to be tracked down or get sucked into some FBI scam."

Walt rubbed his head, sighing with every pass. "None of this makes any sense."

Frustration filled Jonas. This man's opinion meant something. He'd been involved in every major turning point in

Jonas's life. Having Walt cut Courtney off struck Jonas like a physical blow.

"I was there when the guy tried to kill her, Walt. I'm not abandoning her now."

"You sure you're thinking with your head on this one?"

Jonas refused to answer that. Whatever he felt, and he had no idea what that was, didn't concern anyone else. He could be objective. He could save the girl and figure out the case without compromising his office. "This is about her safety."

"I'm just going to say it." Walt shifted his weight from foot to foot. "I don't trust her one bit. I think she's dirty."

Hearing the words made Jonas ball his hands into fists. The fierce need to fight for her honor struck him out of nowhere. "Walt, come on. She's had a hundred chances to run off or do something to me."

"That's not any kind of comfort."

"How about the fact she's sticking this out despite being terrified?"

Walt paced the small area as he blew out a long breath. "I've known you a long time, and that doesn't sound like you're keeping your distance."

The charge stuck.

Jonas tried to shake it out, convince his brain that the words lacked merit, but the accusation lingered. He had to believe he could separate the case from the woman. "I am."

Walt stopped. "If you do lose perspective, call me. A man in a position of power and protection needs to be objective."

"I get that."

"Then you know once you can't keep your distance, neither of you is safe."

"I have it under control." Jonas glanced at the bloodstain on the floor and hoped that was true.

Chapter Twelve

Less than a half hour later, Courtney stood in a parking lot and stared at two buildings arranged in an L shape. Each consisted of two stories.

The place sat just outside the Aberdeen city line. The sign out front said Happy Times Apartments and advertised nightly rentals. The place looked more like a motel out of a horror movie to her.

Rows of doors and small windows stood every few feet. A staircase ran down from the second floor on each end of both buildings. The too-blue paint failed to stick to the stucco underneath, leaving big blotches of lime-green visible, which matched the color of the pool in the middle.

She cringed at the idea of sleeping here. "This isn't the safe house, is it?"

Jonas stopping eyeing up the dark blue sedan parked under the sign that said Management Office and stared at her. "What?"

"You know, where we stay while we're in hiding. Don't mean to sound like a princess or anything, but this isn't it, is it?"

A smile tugged at the corner of his mouth. "We're staying at my house."

She wasn't sure if that news comforted or terrified her. A

warm shower and a soft bed—all good. A room just down the hall from his? Trouble.

She hadn't had a steady boyfriend since college, and they broke up when he pushed to meet her family and she wasn't ready to tell him there wasn't anyone else. The one man since meant nothing, and she'd regretted it the minute she let the relationship slip from casual and work-related to something more.

Then Jonas knocked on her door, and long-dead feelings inside her sparked to life. Or they had the second she stopped running from him.

Hearing his steady breathing the night before soothed her to sleep. Her usual insomnia gave way to her body's need to heal from all the violence. But part of her worried this was something else.

"Then why are we here?" she asked.

"Ron Stimpson lives up there." Jonas pointed at the middle door on the second floor of the closest building.

"Remind me who he is again."

"The guard who left his post at Eckert's door."

"Bartholomew County needs to pay its sheriffs more money." She glanced at the man-size hole in the metal fence surrounding the pool. "This place is a dump."

"He's divorced. The wife and kid have the house. He has a money-flow problem."

"Did you know the guy or something?"

Jonas slipped his phone out of his back pocket and hit a few buttons. "Rich texted the information."

She read the screen Jonas showed her. "So, do we think Stimpson just messed up and left?"

"No."

She knew the answer before Jonas said it but the why still eluded her. "Care to elaborate?"

"It's too coincidental."

Yeah, much clearer now. But as someone who lived under the crushing weight of a false accusation, she refused to jump in and blame. "Maybe the person who killed Eckert waited until the guard stepped away."

"Then the killer would have been hanging out on the hospital floor for some period of time." Jonas shook his head. "The risk of getting caught on tape or by the personnel would be too high."

"So you're not buying it."

"It's one thing to get lost in the shuffle of business on a hospital floor. It's another to wait around, trying to act like you belong."

"So Stimpson was dirty." The idea shouldn't have surprised her. She'd dealt with lazy cops and more than a few guys in power who seemed to despise women. But she'd hoped for better here, had the naive belief that sort of corruption wouldn't happen in a small town on the edge of nowhere.

"He wouldn't be the first bad cop in history."

The disgust in Jonas's voice mirrored the anger in her heart. "Interesting."

He pocketed his phone. "What?"

"The way you got all low and grumbly there for a second."

"I didn't—"

"And if you hold on to those keys any tighter you're going to draw blood."

He opened his palm and stared at the rough indents on his palm.

"Have some experience with crooked officers?" she asked.

He hesitated long enough that his voice boomed and she jumped when he finally started talking. "Most of the people on the streets, the true law-enforcement professionals who sweat and bleed the beat each day, are solid. They do their jobs. Risk their lives. Don't ask for medals."

Like him. After such a short time, that was the definition she'd use to describe Jonas.

"I know plenty of guys who sit behind a desk and give orders. They dictate the rules of battle without ever fighting one," he said.

Desperate to hear him talk, to catch a glimpse into the man behind the fully together one in front of her, she resisted saying anything until the quiet pounded in on her. "And?"

"People die."

It was everything he didn't say that mattered. "People you know?"

"Yeah." He dangled the keys in front of her. "These are for you."

The air had changed. The crackle of electricity vanished in a poof and she knew the "show me yours" moment had passed.

She sighed. "Let me guess. My job is to wait out here."

"In the car with the engine running."

"Where will you be?"

"Up there." He nodded toward Stimpson's front door before looking over his shoulder at the sedan again. "The guy in that car is one of Walt's men. He's watching the place to see if Stimpson comes back."

"I'm confused about this plan."

Jonas shrugged. "I'm just looking in some windows."

"Guess that means you don't have a warrant."

"Walt is getting it. He'll be here any minute."

She rolled her eyes. "Oh, good. And I thought you were running off without backup again."

For a second the tight pull of tension across his mouth disappeared and he laughed. "Only a crazy man would do that." Amusement echoed in every word.

"I had the same thought."

Jonas winked at her, then waved to the officer in the car.

He headed for the stairs on the left side of the building. He hit the bottom one before she decided helping him look in a few windows couldn't put her in danger.

She'd barely raised her leg when the ground shook beneath her. A deafening crash thundered through the sky and rattled in her ears. Her knees buckled as the pavement bounced and shifted.

One minute she saw Jonas's shirt. The next he flew backward as the railing in his hand broke free and the stairs blew apart. She tried to call his name but no words came out. Smoke choked the air and glass rained from above.

Car alarms exploded in unison with chirping sounds. People screamed and a baby cried. The roar of drums sounded all around her.

She hit her knees and threw her hands over her head. Sharp pricks assaulted her bare skin as she hid her face. She didn't know she'd held her breath until her chest burned and she started coughing.

Her eyes itched and watered as if the smoke had worked its way under her contacts, but the raging heat had her full attention. Fire danced all around her. Flames engulfed the top floor of the complex except in the black hole in the middle. Papers flew around. Pieces of furniture littered the ground. And the sedan with Walt's provided protection burned.

The thumping of her heart and rush of the fire muffled other sounds. She pushed up, ignoring the slice of glass into her palm. Residents stumbled out of the bottom units. Others lay on the ground not moving.

So many people hurt… *Jonas.*

Her vision blurred as the smoke fell over her. She blinked and rubbed her eyes to bring the images back together. When she could focus again, she scanned the ground, trying to remember the last place she saw him. The stairs, the walls, they were gone now, but the fire inched closer and the wind kicked up.

Something moved off to her left. Dark pants. A hand. Jonas lay on his stomach with his face turned away from her.

She struggled to stand up but her legs wouldn't hold her. She slipped back to the ground with a whoosh. Forcing her eyes to focus, she made out Jonas's lean frame and saw the flames edging closer.

She crawled on her elbows and knees, ignoring the crunch of glass as she went. When she got close she reached out and wrapped her fingers around his ankle. He didn't move at her touch. Climbing, shuffling her body along the hard ground, she slid up his body and pressed a finger to his neck. A steady heartbeat greeted her.

With her hands on his back, she shook him and shouted his name. On the third shove, he groaned.

"Jonas, please, wake up." She continued to poke and prod. They had only minutes before the fire reached them. "Come on."

His eyes popped open. "Bomb."

Relief zapped her strength. She fell against him and buried her face in his neck. "We have to move."

"Are you okay?" His question came out in pants.

She lifted her head and brushed a hand over his blackened cheek. "Fine."

"Everyone else?"

"I don't know. Can you get up?"

"I doubt it." He shifted his head and faced the fire. "Forget that. Yeah, I can."

He pushed up on his forearms, his arms shaking as he went. When he pushed back on his knees, his chest heaved.

Panic swamped her. Every cell in her body shook. "Jonas, please."

He opened his eyes again and some of the haze had cleared. "Let's go. I can come back for the others."

She doubted he could even rescue himself this time.

With her arms wrapped around him and his weight suffocating her, they half crouched and half crawled out of the line of the fire. Sirens wailed in the distance, growing louder. She laughed, so relieved by the welcome noise.

They were a few steps from freedom when strong arms reached under her stomach and pulled her away. She screamed out Jonas's name and kicked out her legs.

Then the smoke closed around her.

Chapter Thirteen

Jonas moved his arms but he wasn't holding anything but air. He blinked several times to clear his vision as he called Courtney's name over and over again.

He could hear her screams over the blaring whistle of the incoming fire trucks. As the wind blew, a patch of visibility opened and he saw a man dragging Courtney away. The man had his arms banded around her chest as she dug in her heels to stop him.

If she could find the power to fight, so could he. Jonas crawled until he struggled up on all fours, willing his body to keep moving. He fell twice, but on the third try he rose up on shaky legs.

The smoke had blown back in, and heat seared his back. He turned to find the fire creeping in a line toward him. Adrenaline surged through him, coursing through his blood and shooting power back into his beaten muscles.

The window of smoke closed and he couldn't see her anymore. "Courtney!"

"Jonas, here!"

He followed the sound to a car parked on the opposite side of the complex. Through the thick smoke, Courtney fought, swinging her legs and punching at her attacker. When he tried to open the passenger side and stuff her in, she smacked the door shut by balancing her feet against the side of the car.

Jonas inhaled and ran. His heel overturned, but he kept moving. With a yell, he launched his body at the attacker, hitting him square in the back. The men went down, rolling on the ground, as Courtney's shoulder slammed into the car.

The burst of strength used up all of Jonas's reserves. He coughed through the smoke as he struggled to see the face of the guy shoving him harder into the pavement. All Jonas could think about was getting to Courtney and carrying her out of there and finding help for the others.

He shoved and hit. Then the guy was gone. The pressure lifted, and without the knee on his chest Jonas's breathing slowed again.

He lay on the pavement staring up at the now-dark sky clouded with a thick film. Then Courtney's face swirled in front of him, her hair streaming down and her skin damp with sweat. She was saying something but he couldn't hear her. Her mouth moved.

The ground vibrated. At first he only saw shoes. Hoses hit the ground around him. Rich swooped in, taking Courtney by the shoulders and wrapping her in a blanket.

Jonas blinked as firemen and police poured through the area from every direction. With a hard pop, his ears opened. He heard the spray of water and Walt's shouts for help.

Then thick air swept over him with the darkness roaring in right behind.

When Jonas opened his eyes again, he saw ceiling tiles. Rows of white and nothing familiar. He lifted his head and scanned the room. Heart-rate monitor, a thin sheet drawn up to his stomach and a bed with rails.

He exhaled, his breath filled with fury. "I'm in a damn hospital."

"Yes, you are."

His gaze shot to the chair next to his bed. Courtney sat in jeans and a T-shirt, with her legs tucked up under her and a magazine on her lap. Her skin was pink and shiny, and her hair was pulled back off her face.

"You're okay." He meant to say the words in his head, but when she smiled he knew he'd said them out loud.

She held up her hand and showed off a white bandage. "Minor stuff."

He looked closer and saw the dark circles and tiny cuts on her forehead and hands. Her left eye watered and she rubbed it twice in the minute since he woke up and saw her. Her elbow balanced on the armrest but her whole side moved when she did, suggesting an injury to her ribs and maybe her arm and back.

She was hurt.

He tried to get up and his chest caved in. Coughs shook him until he couldn't see. When he leaned back again, Rich and Courtney loomed over him wearing matching looks of concern.

Jonas hated pity. After his partner got shot, everyone in his division at DEA stopped talking when he walked by. There were whispers and awkward private comments about getting a raw deal.

He'd gone from an excellent shot to the guy who failed to pull the trigger on time. From being on probation over an innocent incident in one case to forced temporary leave over another. He knew how to shoot and when to shoot, but the bogus lawsuit over the kid left him questioning his judgment, and in that second months later his partner paid the price.

Henry McCarthy, dead at thirty-one.

"Tell me what happened today," Jonas said.

"It's simple." Rich stationed his body at the end of Jonas's bed. "Someone blew up Stimpson's house and tried to take you with it."

Knowing people were hurt and in trouble while he was

strapped to a bed ate at Jonas's insides, hollowing him out. "Injuries?"

"Stimpson is dead. We're not sure if the fire killed him or covered up the homicide."

"Everyone else?"

"The officer in the sedan." Courtney swallowed the last part of the sentence. She clamped her lips together as if the idea of saying one more word pained her.

Rich cleared his throat. "It happened during the day, so most people were out. We have some folks in the hospital but nothing life-threatening."

"You're one of the worst," she said, the anger clear in her voice.

Rich nodded. "And you look like crap."

Jonas didn't care about that. He'd been injured before, spent time in the army and tracked down drug dealers with the DEA. He was in good shape. His body would heal.

The damage to Aberdeen might not be as easily fixed. People here expected calm and safety. He'd been on the job six months and delivered the exact opposite.

But the bigger issue had to do with the woman standing by his side. "What about the guy who took Courtney? Any idea who he is or where he went?"

"Good Samaritan, maybe?" Rich threw it out there but his eyes said he didn't believe it.

She snorted. "More like kidnapper."

"And this used to be a nice place to live," Rich joked.

She slipped back into the chair and rubbed her eyes. "Before I got here, you mean."

Rich sobered. "No, before a killer came to town."

Jonas watched the byplay. Where Walt sent out warning signals, Rich stepped into protection mode with Courtney. Jonas appreciated both tactics but neither would keep her safe. They needed more information. Fighting the unknown had proven too dangerous for everyone in town.

"Can you describe him?" Jonas asked her.

She rubbed her hands up and down her arms. "He grabbed me from behind. I didn't see anything."

Jonas tipped his head back against the pillow and closed his eyes. He tried to conjure up a view of the guy, but couldn't. For all his training, his skills failed when he needed them most. "And I was too busy trying to get to you to concentrate on getting a description."

"And then there's the part where you were almost unconscious." She reached out a hand but laid it on the railing instead of touching him.

His gaze went to her fingers before skipping back to Rich and his stupid smile. Jonas wondered if he'd ever regain his equilibrium. He had a job to do, but his performance suffered whenever she walked by.

He shook his head and tried to get his mind back on track. "What do we know?"

"You need to stay in here for a few..." Rich raised an eyebrow. "Why are you shaking your head?"

Never going to happen. "I'm leaving as soon as the doctor signs the papers."

This time Courtney wrapped her fingers around the metal bar to his bed in a hold tight enough to crush it. "We don't even know what's wrong with you."

"I can think of a few things," Rich said.

Jonas ignored both of them. "How long have I been in here?"

Rich glanced at his watch before answering. "Most of the day."

"And you?" Jonas asked Courtney.

"Sitting right here, except when I was next door."

"I didn't leave her side when the doctor checked her over." Rich gave the explanation before Jonas's furor could explode.

"Except when I showered."

That was the last thing Jonas wanted to think about. Actually, if he was honest, he had to admit it was near the top of his list. The need to protect her and kiss her had merged until he couldn't separate one from the other.

He had no idea how he'd ever survive being alone with her, but he didn't have a choice because he was not going anywhere. "We'll head back to my house—"

"You should stay here. I'm not leaving, and if for some reason I have to head out, Walt has agreed to stay and watch over Courtney." Rich raised his voice as Jonas shook his head. "We're not trusting anyone else to watch over the two of you."

Jonas pushed down the covers until he realized he wore nothing more than a hospital gown. When he pinned Rich down for some answers, he'd add how he got naked to the list.

"We're leaving," Jonas said.

Courtney crossed her arms over her stomach and smiled up at Rich. "Told you he'd say that."

Jonas glanced at both of them. "What?"

Rich shrugged. "She bet me you'd insist on leaving."

Jonas choked, this time unrelated to smoke. "You took that bet?"

Rich shrugged. "She'd had a hard day. I threw her one."

Jonas pressed the buzzer for the nurse. "Hand me my clothes. I have a job and some investigating to do. End of conversation."

"Guess Walt and I will be taking turns watching your house instead of hanging out here." Rich pulled a bag out of the closet and placed it on the bed in front of Jonas.

"We'll be fine." He unsnapped the top and dumped the contents on the bed. "Where is everything else?"

Courtney stood up and scanned the items. "What do you mean?"

"Wallet. Keys. Gun." He dropped each item on the mattress as he did the inventory. "Where's my cell?"

"It probably fell out during the blast." Courtney moved the things around. "Or when you wrestled with that guy."

Jonas looked at Rich. "Check the scene."

"What are you thinking here?" Rich asked.

"I don't know." But Jonas's brain kicked into gear. For everything else to be there except his phone didn't make sense. Having something personal in the hands of someone who didn't think twice about tackling a police officer made the nerve in his neck throb.

"Can we get back to the part where you think you're leaving?" Courtney's eyebrow lifted as she spoke.

"No. Let's get you home so I can check on Walt."

Courtney grumbled something about men being idiots. "I want to be clear that I think this is a bad idea. You should stay here."

Jonas didn't necessarily disagree with her. "Noted."

Chapter Fourteen

His craziness was making her paranoid.

After spending what felt like an hour locking the doors and windows of his house, Jonas picked up the new phone he'd grabbed from work and talked with people about the explosion. He gave instructions and revised work schedules. He'd even lectured the sheriff stationed on the street about how best to conduct surveillance on the house.

Only after Jonas traded texts with Rich about the status of the investigation and any leads did he finally sit. But he didn't stop. He lectured her about staying away from the windows. She listened, hoping he would wear his brain out and drift off to sleep. He finally did.

Now she sat on one end of the sectional sofa and watched him sprawled across the other. Blankets piled in the middle where their feet met. His chest rose and fell in natural breaths. Dark eyelashes touched against the tops of his cheeks.

Even in sleep he looked ready to pounce. Pillows propped him up and a gun lay in easy reach underneath the couch.

When she touched a foot against his and he didn't move, she took the opportunity to look around. He'd hustled her in here and ran through the floor plan and identified the exits, telling her to memorize everything. Rich had stayed at her back while Jonas checked every cabinet, every last inch of the place.

Now she could see it was an older two-story farmhouse surrounded by trees. The peeling paint and creaky boards on the porch gave it a rustic look. Inside, the floors were clean and the furnishings minimal and dark. White walls, navy sofa and no clutter, except for the dining room that Jonas had set up as a makeshift wood shop.

He'd explained he was in midrenovation. With his work schedule, she guessed it would take a decade to finish, but it had potential. The rooms were large with built-ins and beautiful trim. The yard was nice and deep.

The perfect family house being occupied by a bachelor. She had no idea if that meant something.

She laid her head against the cushions and closed her eyes. The edges burned and the one would not stop watering. Even without reading and looming over her workstation, the fatigue had set in. She'd have to put on the glasses soon. That would test Jonas's theory about men making passes.

Not that he'd been all that subtle on the subject. He'd been dropping small hints, a stray comment here and there, that let her know about his interest level. A gentle touch against her shoulder to get her attention or a glance that caressed as it swept over her face, both so in contrast with his size and strength.

The mysterious tough-guy type never appealed to her. Oh, she liked to look because men like that did have the best shoulders, but the idea of a relationship with a guy who could bench-press a car made her feel the exact opposite of safe. Physically strong men could inflict pain. She couldn't fight back if someone like that used his fists.

Her gaze traveled over Jonas's hand where it lay on his stomach, just touching his belt. Lean fingers, the same ones he'd spread across her back.

She waited for the fear and disgust to bubble up but it never happened. Jonas's hands made her think about fingertips brushing over bare skin. About heat and light.

A crash like the sound of metal on metal brought her mind flying back to the present. Her feet hit the floor as she sat up and stared through the doorway to the back of the house.

The police were outside. Jonas had set the alarm. The sound was nothing more than a trash can. She repeated the explanation, trying to convince her mind to accept it, until she heard the noise a second time.

She leaned over with her upper body resting on Jonas's thighs. "Wake up."

His hand slipped into her hair as his legs shifted to give her more space.

"Jonas." Her whisper bordered on frantic now. She couldn't keep that anxiety from crashing over her and coming out in her voice. "Please, get up."

His body stilled as his hand dropped to his side. "I'm not sleeping."

"We have a problem."

"What?" The sleepiness hadn't faded from his voice.

"I hear something."

His eyes popped open as he struggled to sit up despite her weight pushing him into the cushions. "Where?"

"Out back, upstairs. I don't really know."

He eased her off of him and sat up, slipping his feet into the sneakers he'd left by the couch. "Describe it."

"A bang." She tried to call it up from memory but couldn't. Fear made her dizzy. "It could have been the wind, but I thought someone was trying to get in."

"That's definitely a problem." He stood up in a fluid movement, feet on the floor and a gun in his hand. No limping or groaning.

No one would ever guess what his body had been through over the past two days. He controlled each muscle with ease.

"Give me a direction," he said.

She called up a diagram in her head, but locating the source after the fact proved tough. She thought she knew, but wasn't willing to risk his life on a maybe. "Call for backup. Let someone else skulk around out there in the dark."

"If someone is in here, the silent alarm has been tripped." He reached down and swiped his phone off the coffee table.

The tapping of his fingers against the screen screamed like a freight train through the room. She knew it was her imagination, but the walls closed in, anyway.

He tucked the phone into his back pocket. "And now the not-so-silent alarm is going off at the station. They should be here in a minute since the station is right around the corner."

The idea of carloads of police officers descending on the property actually appealed to her. Since meeting Jonas she welcomed law enforcement into her life. Well, some.

She slipped her fingers under his elbow and prepared for a verbal battle waged in hushed tones. "We should get out of here."

Instead, he nodded. "Agreed."

His answer stunned her. He was the race-in-and-solve-it type. Several times since she'd met him, the world fell apart and he worked alone to get it up and spinning again. This time he used common sense.

She was immediately suspicious. "What are you doing?"

He pushed her behind him and covered her as they walked backward to the front door. "Getting you out of here."

"You're coming with me?"

"Yes."

She grabbed on to the back of his shirt. "Why aren't you fighting me?"

"I'm trying to be realistic."

"Not what I was expecting."

"My body is done. Taking this threat on alone could get us both killed." He stole a quick look out the narrow window that ran parallel to the front door. "And, believe it or not, I'd like to go an hour or two without a homicide on my watch."

Doubt nibbled at the edges of her brain. "Maybe I imagined it."

"No." He slipped an arm by her and turned the knob. "I believe you."

The door opened and a cool, damp wind pressed against her back. As soon as her feet landed on the porch, Jonas signaled to the guy in the sheriff's car. The guy shut the door and shot across the lawn toward them.

"What's wrong?" The man scanned the yard with wide eyes as he walked up the wide front steps.

Jonas tried to set her away from him. "Put Ms. Allen in your car."

She kept her death grip on his arm. "You promised."

"I actually didn't, but I'm not going in alone." He waved for the sheriff to come closer. "Someone is in the house."

The guy froze in midstep. "But how—"

Four police cars raced down the street with sirens blaring and lights flashing. The noise was enough to bring every neighbor running. Front doors opened and people spilled out onto their porches and driveways.

The familiar scene had Courtney's head spinning. People talking and watching. All the judging and questions, and once again much of it aimed in her direction. Her mind spun until it landed on that night years ago.

"This is different." Jonas whispered the thought against her ear.

"I know." She swallowed back the choking anxiety and tried to focus on the positive. The show of neighbor support might be a good thing. Anything to scare the intruder away worked for her.

But Jonas didn't stay calm, either. He exhaled and swore at the same time. "Damn."

"What is it?"

"The guys were supposed to come in quiet." Jonas glanced up at his second floor. "We'll never catch the intruder now."

Rich jogged up the lawn with two officers right behind. "Now what?"

Jonas whipped around then pressed his hand to the bandage on his forehead. "Potential intruder."

"Did your alarm go off?" When Jonas gave a short shake of his head, Rich tried again. "Did you see him?"

"I heard him." She stared at the police and sheriff cars clogging the street. She counted eight. "But you'll get him, right? I mean, how does he get past all of this?"

"I have a feeling he's gone." Jonas blew out a harsh breath then started pointing. "Okay, surround the house. We need to go in hard. Someone is in there."

Before she could protest, Rich jumped in. "You mean *we* need to. You're staying here."

Jonas made a noise that sounded a lot like a growl. "Rich—"

"I'm overruling you on this and you know I'm right." Rich turned around and motioned for the policemen to gather around.

"Fine," Jonas said through clenched teeth before he pushed his way into the center of the circle.

He issued clear, short orders in seconds. When he lifted his head again, the men spread out. They all wore vests and carried guns. Groups of two went around each side of the house. Rich and another man she didn't recognize slipped through the front door, one after the other, all while Jonas talked on police radios about blocking the street and clearing out the neighbors for their safety.

When he looked back at his house, a nerve twitched in his cheek. She knew standing on the sidelines killed him. For a man like Jonas, watching ripped against the grain. He didn't send in another man to fight his battles. He waded in on his own.

She admired that. Admired almost everything about him, actually.

She heard shouts from inside the house. "I hope I didn't imagine it."

He finally glanced at her. "Do you think you did?"

"I honestly don't know anymore, Jonas. So much has happened in the past two days."

He wrapped an arm around her shoulders and pulled her in tight against his side. With his mouth close to her ear, he whispered, "I trust you."

The word zinged right to her heart. She searched her mind, tried to remember if anyone had ever said that to her. Not since she turned twenty. She'd spent many years throwing out theories and ideas about her father and people discounted them. Except for her work, where she ruled with a soft hand and no one questioned her, she expected people not to listen to her.

Rich stepped out onto the porch, his boots clomping against the old wood. "Jonas, there's no one in there."

Her stomach fell. "I'm sorry."

"Don't be." Jonas squeezed her shoulder before his arm dropped. "Anything missing?"

"You'll have to check, but nothing obvious." Rich marched down the steps, ripping the Velcro on his vest as he went.

She was desperate for Rich not to see her as a crazy person. "I swear I heard it."

When he looked at her, his expression went blank. "I'll put another man on the house and take the night shift myself."

She shook her head. "I'm sorry."

Rich snorted. "You have reason to be on edge after the thing in the forest."

"But this?"

He winked at her. "So long as it doesn't happen every hour, we're fine."

Jonas clapped Rich on the shoulder. "Thanks for racing here."

"Per your orders, I have patrols going through town. Walt stepped up and provided additional personnel."

"I owe him."

"He mentioned that."

More men poured out of the house and headed for the cars. She was trying to figure out a new way to apologize when a younger policeman came around the side of the house and waved to Jonas. "I think we have something here, sir."

Rich and Jonas took off and Courtney followed them. The group stopped at the small window over the kitchen sink. Jonas ran his hand over the sill.

"What is it?" Rich asked.

"Marks in the wood."

Rich made a face as he eyed the chipped paint. "How can you tell?"

"See this?" Jonas pointed to a thin scrape at the bottom of the window and near the lock at the top. "This isn't from disrepair. Someone tried to work this open."

She stared at the tight space. "Even if he did get it open, who could fit through there?"

"Good question." Jonas pointed at the officer who found the marks. "Good job. I doubt we'll find anything, but we need a fingerprint kit."

The guy almost tripped over his own feet running to do Jonas's bidding.

Rich watched and shook his head. "I'll set up roadblocks and start a search. The guy is likely long gone, but it's worth a shot."

Jonas nodded. "Right."

"Do we have any idea why someone wants to get to you so badly?" Rich asked her.

She debated on how much to share. "Well—"

Jonas made the decision for her. "I'll fill you in later."

"Then I'll go handle the basics." Rich turned the corner and disappeared.

Standing alone at the back of the house, Courtney shivered from the chilling wind. A few seconds ago she hadn't even felt it.

Jonas frowned at her. "You okay?"

She rubbed her hands over her arms and felt the tiny bumps there. "Fine, but I'm trying to believe you're not furious about someone violating your space."

"Don't let the calm fool you. My biggest goal is to figure out how someone got this close to you without me knowing it."

Having her back exposed had her shifting to lean against the house. "That one has me worried, too."

"They won't be back."

She closed her sore eye and peeked up at him with the other. "How do you know that? I don't care what the answer is. I just want reassurance. Tell me you're sure."

"It's easy." He pressed a palm against the house, right next to her head, and leaned in. "He knows we're ready."

"What if what the person really wants is me?"

"The only one who's going to be near you is me."

The trembling inside her had nothing to do with the cold. "I'm not sure how to take that."

He drew even closer, with his mouth just inches from hers. For a second, she thought he would close the distance and kiss her. Instead, he pushed off and stood up.

"Yeah, you do."

"Jonas—"

He held out a hand to her. "Let's go see what Rich is doing."

Chapter Fifteen

Cade sat on the hood of his rental car and let the heat from the metal warm him from the wind whipping across the Siuslaw River. He blew out long breaths, trying to restore his heart to a consistent beat.

The call had come in less than an hour ago. The county sheriff hit Redial on Paul's phone and called Cade. At first, Cade kept it all business, ready to deliver the cover he'd created for Paul's trip. Then came the news. The sheriff filled Cade in as a law-enforcement courtesy.

Paul was dead. Killed in the hospital room.

Thinking about his friend's slashed throat made Cade gag again. He'd thrown up twice since he got off the phone. Wiping the sweat off his forehead, Cade counted to ten as he opened his mouth and gulped in fresh air.

He'd been right there in the room.

He'd dragged Paul into this mess.

Cade rubbed his hands up and down his pants legs but his skin wouldn't warm up. The cold penetrated every cell. Whether it came from reaction or shock, he didn't know. The result was the same. Someone murdered his friend. The same unknown someone managed to get the jump on a trained FBI agent.

The impact would reach everywhere. Color everything. Destroy so much.

Cade inhaled again, trying to keep the clog in his throat from coming up. Watching the blue water lap against the bank and the gray sky move in, his thoughts moved from one death to another.

Tad Willis had collapsed under the weight of the accusations. He didn't fight. He gave in. Ann or Courtney, or whatever her name was these days, picked him as the killer and told everyone. The reporters called day and night. Neighbors painted words of hate on their garage door. Kids taunted.

The past Cade's father tried so hard to hide boiled up and became an explanation for how he could wipe out an entire family. Being short on cash no longer stood as the household's most devastating problem.

Cade's regular world had exploded when his father's name appeared in the papers. After a raging fight at the dinner table, he skipped out on school the next morning, snuck home and found his dad's body in the bedroom.

The gun. The blood. The shocking red covered everything. The way it dripped down the wall, Cade thought it had to be paint. It signaled the end of his innocence and his father's life.

Now there was more blood. Cade looked down expecting to see it drip off his hands. Paul had an ex-wife and a new fiancée. He'd had a life.

Cade's thoughts wandered back to Courtney. He could trace every piece-of-crap thing in his life back to her. He brought Paul to town but Courtney, or something related to her, killed him.

She'd taken enough lives. She had to be stopped.

JONAS SAT at his dining-room table and tapped his pen against the wood. The rhythmic clicking soothed him. Exhaustion tugged at every bone in his body, but he fought it off. He needed answers. Courtney needed answers.

As if he conjured her up, she slipped into the room. She'd showered again, and the dampness still clung to the ends of her hair. Her navy sweats balanced low on her slim hips, teasing him with a sliver of skin between the edge and the bottom of her body-skimming T-shirt.

This time she wore glasses. The thin, dark frames gave her a naughty-librarian look.

He hadn't been kidding when he said glasses were sexy on a woman. Or maybe he just thought it and forgot to actually tell her. Either way, he believed it.

"You dream about being a drummer?" she asked with a wide smile.

"What?"

She made exaggerated googly eyes at his pen. "Can't place the beat, but I'll probably hear that sound in my sleep."

"Sorry about that. One of the hazards of being a bachelor and living alone."

"It's okay." She sat in the chair perpendicular to his with one leg tucked under her. "I doubt I'll actually sleep no matter how quiet you are."

And he'd almost fallen asleep pouring his coffee. "After all that's happened, how could you not?"

She shrugged as she drew a random pattern on the table with her finger. "I don't need that many hours."

"Need? It's about how good it feels."

She glanced up at him. "Oh, really?"

"Soft, warm." He saw her breathing slow and heard the soft puffs of air leave her mouth. "After it's over, your body is restored and ready to go."

Her finger stalled. "Are we still talking about sleeping?"

Not even a little. "Sort of."

The chair creaked when she flopped against the back. "About this attraction."

That woke him right up. "I'm impressed you opened that topic."

"I'm not wrong about… Well." She swung her leg around in a circle. "I thought—"

"It's taking all the control I have not to get up and bend you over the table. Does that answer your question on how I feel and how mutual this is?"

Her body froze. "Pretty much."

"So?"

"You're not my type. I'm guessing I'm not yours."

He leaned back until the front two legs of his chair left the floor. "Wrong."

"You like the bookish girls?"

She had no idea of her appeal. For the first time, he understood she lost more than her family that awful night long ago. He wondered if she realized how hard she was on herself. "I'm into the strong-and-pretty type."

"Do I fall into that category?"

"You're the star of it."

"Men with guns make me nervous." Her fingers wound together on her lap. She folded and unfolded them, her hands in constant motion.

"I get that."

"To break the panic, I took some lessons and spent some time on a shooting range."

Nothing about her surprised him. Rather than get swamped by fear, she fought it. It's what he would have done. His admiration grew along with his attraction.

"Did it help?" he asked.

"The hyperventilating is gone. I can watch a shoot-'em-up movie without throwing up."

His gun was a part of him. Holding it was as natural as breathing, but he never forgot its power. "But seeing a real one is different."

"Yeah, so was holding one. I expected something small and light."

"Guns are heavy."

Her chest lifted on a deep exhale. "I've had bad luck with police officers and people connected to the legal system."

"What about me?" His chair fell to the floor with a thump.

"What?"

"What kind of luck have you had with me?"

Her fingers turned red from where she rubbed and twisted them. "Since I've almost gotten you killed several times, I'm thinking you should run away and keep going until I'm nothing more than a bad memory."

"I'm not going anywhere."

Her head dropped back and she stared at the ceiling. In that moment he found two more things about her that he wanted to touch and taste: a long neck and the sharp line of her jaw.

When she lowered her head again, her eyes burned with a fiery intensity. "I keep waiting to see the thing, that part of you that will scare me to death."

The way her voice dipped went straight to the heaviness in his chest. "I'm not going to lie to you. I'm not perfect, and I've made huge mistakes in my life, but I won't hurt you."

"I think that's what scares me."

Not the words he expected. "I don't get it."

"I know." She laughed. "I don't, either."

"Is it a guy thing?"

The smile still lit her eyes. "Far as I can tell, there's nothing wrong with your guy thing."

The pressure constricting his upper body relaxed. "Then what's holding you back?"

"Nothing."

She was on him then, up and out of the chair, meeting him in the middle between their seats. Her hands roamed over his back as their mouths met in the kiss he'd been fantasizing about since he met her.

Deep and hot, her lips covered his. Over and over he pressed, bringing her body in close. Feeling her, tasting her.

With his hands on her hips, he lifted her onto the table and slipped into the V of her legs. His coffee cup clanked as it fell and papers slipped to the floor. He shoved the boxes aside to give them room, all without breaking contact with her sexy mouth.

Her chest brushed against his as his hands tunneled up the back of her shirt to touch bare skin. The feel of her smooth flesh had him lifting her T-shirt up and off. Breaths pounded in his chest as his hands closed over her breasts. Without a bra as a barrier, tight nipples brushed across his palms as he cupped her.

She whipped her glasses off and let them fall to the side. "Yes."

He leaned his forehead against hers as the blood rushed out of his head. He wanted her so much. He craved her.

"You feel so good." He whispered the words against her lips.

She traced circles over his chest with her hands. "My turn."

The smokiness of her voice contrasted with the cool temperature of the room. The chilled air hit him the second she shoved his shirt up and off.

When he came back to her, his body on fire against hers, he found her mouth again. Their breathing mixed. Their tongues touched. Every ounce of control shattered as the reasons to stay away from her drifted out of his head.

He licked her lips and started nibbling on the edge of her mouth. "We should go upstairs."

She shook her head and mumbled something. He couldn't hear her over the waves of blood crashing in his head. He trailed a line of kisses down her neck to the promising dip at the base of her throat. When her head drifted back and a tiny moan escaped her lips, he knew he'd found the right spot.

When her fingers went to work on his belt, he also knew they needed a bed. "Upstairs."

He grabbed her hand and tugged her off the table. Or he tried to. She wouldn't budge.

"Courtney?"

She dug in her small back pocket and pulled out a condom. "We have this." She waved it in front of his face. "Found it in your bathroom."

"Aren't you enterprising?"

"You've accused me of that before."

He took the packet and had to control his hands to keep from shredding the thing. "It was a compliment both times."

She opened the buttons on his jeans with an aching slowness. One by one, they popped open as her fingers brushed against him. By the time she finished, his lower body thumped with the need to be inside her. And when she slipped her hand over him, he saw black spots behind his eyes.

His breath hiccupped in his chest. "I'm not going to be able to handle this for very long."

She pressed her lips against his ear. "Good."

The last hold on sanity snapped. He lowered her to the table, his body sliding against hers as she opened her legs. He stood up long enough to strip the pants and underwear down her legs. When he touched her, felt how ready she was for him, her back arched off the top.

He wanted to make this good. Make it last. But his body had other ideas.

A rip echoed through the room as he opened the packet

and rolled the condom on. Then he was inside of her and nothing else mattered. He felt her under him and around him.

When she tightened her legs and begged him to move, he stopped thinking at all.

Chapter Sixteen

Kurt dialed the number a second time, his anger festering with each button he punched. When the fourth ring turned to voice mail, he threw the expensive phone against the passenger door and watched it bounce to the floor.

He was not a man other people ignored. He wielded power and could shut off access on a whim. He rarely did because a smart businessman didn't let his ego edge out a good deal. His job was to make money, and he dealt with whomever he needed to in order to make that happen.

But he had a long memory. Having someone on his payroll pretend he didn't exist ticked him off.

Kurt glanced across the street and stared at the front door of the modest ranch house then back to the car parked in front of the garage. Kurt had seen the other man go in there a half hour earlier. It was eight at night and the guy was off shift. He wasn't out. Even if he hadn't heard the first call, he had a chance to pick up the second.

The man's job required that he be tied to a phone, and there was no way he took the night off. Not with everything happening in the area.

Kurt tapped his fingers against the glass and searched for a logical explanation for the sudden vocal blackout. Nothing acceptable came to him. Maybe the job got too rough.

Maybe the man thought ten thousand dollars only bought a security tape and a few seconds of a guard's time.

Kurt disagreed. His pack of money bought access and an assistant, willing or not. Kurt took care of Stimpson to send a message to his suddenly reluctant helper. If even someone with a brief connection to Kurt was expendable, the other man should get the hint and straighten out.

He should answer when he got an important call.

Kurt stared at his phone where it lay on the floor. When the panel stayed dark, the fury whipped around inside him. His skin heated and his teeth ached from the way he held his jaw.

He hit his fist against the car window. By the third smack, the side of his hand was raw but his mind jump-started.

Enough waiting. The timing was perfect, and he couldn't even take any credit for it. He needed Courtney. Cade Willis being in town provided the perfect cover.

All Kurt had to do was get the girl, then wrap her death around Cade's neck and sink him with it.

But first Kurt had to get his paid law-enforcement help back in line.

COURTNEY SKIMMED HER BARE LEG across the soft sheets. When she didn't hit a warm male, she sat up.

With the cover pulled up to her chest, she reached across to Jonas's side of the bed and flipped the clock around to face her. She had to squint to read the numbers. Three in the morning. After hours of lovemaking and one or two of sleep, she woke up sore in all the right places, but alone.

She glanced around the near-black room, forcing her eyes to adjust. Huge bed. Open closet doors and a small chest of drawers with a mirror above it on the wall. The window was closed and the bathroom dark.

Everything was exactly as she remembered when she

drifted off to sleep a few hours before. Neat and orderly, nothing extra and everything in its place.

Jonas stepped out of the bathroom. He hadn't turned the light on, so he didn't have to turn it back off again.

He stood there naked. She took a second to drink in the sight of him. Broad shoulders angled down to a trim waist. Muscular legs and arms without an ounce of fat on them. He had the body of a runner, long and lean. He stalked rather than walked, and every step showed his strength.

She thought he was sexy the first time she saw him. Well, more like the second time. The first time she was too busy running.

He looked good in clothes and fine without them. Just watching him move around the room made her stomach perform a little flip-flop dance. She was transported back to those days when her biggest problem was her curfew. She'd get dramatic and slam doors when she didn't get her way.

Jonas flashed her a smile and, like a teen girl getting a coveted hello from her football-player crush, she melted. It was embarrassing, really. She was a grown woman, one who'd lived through desperate days, worried the pain would never end. She should be over this feeling.

Having her throat fill and her heart triple-time its beat when Jonas casually touched her counted as an inconvenience. Screaming his name while he made love to her was as near a guarantee of future heartbreak as she'd ever experienced with a man.

Relationships were about putting a temporary bandage on the loneliness. Getting connected meant opening up your mind and heart to devastation.

No. Thank. You.

"You said your dad was in the navy, right?" She brought her knees up and wrapped her arms around them.

The bed dipped when Jonas sat down next to her. "And I spent six years in the army."

"I guess that sort of experience shapes a guy."

He trailed a finger down her arm. "I can make a bed nice and tight."

"That's quite a skill." She referred more to the way the tiny hairs on her arm lifted when he touched her, but she pretended to talk about the bed thing.

"It's never about the actual bed or the marching or any of the other regimented activities. It's about giving you a way to think. About making everyone the same, breaking them down so you can build them back up and they can perform at top efficiency as a team."

"I'd be terrible at that."

He laughed. "Would be? You *are*. Every time I tell you not to move or to hold back, you ignore me."

"It would have been chivalrous of you to refrain from responding."

"You never listen, but I'm used to it."

"Then you won't be disappointed when it happens again." She leaned into him. "And it will."

"But there are times when following rules keeps people alive."

"I feel like I should salute or something."

He laughed again in a sound so rich and warm. "Yeah, I probably sound like a recruitment poster."

"All I know is the life you describe sounds pretty rigid and rough." She balanced her chin on her knees. "I like comfort."

"I'd take the military over my time in the DEA any day." His face tightened and the relaxation humming through him stopped.

She wanted to reach out and soothe him, but she also needed to hear more. Brushing a hand over his chest would lead to her being on her back on the mattress. Fun, but learning more about the man underneath the badge and orders appealed to her.

"You've made comments before. I'm guessing Los Angeles wasn't your favorite city," she said.

"Not really." He fell back against the pillows with his arms crossed behind his head. He'd stopped talking. It was as if the mention of his past threw the no-sharing switch.

She dropped next to him and curled into his side. One hand slipped onto his chest, rubbing across his skin in the hope of calming him again. Her foot inched up his calf.

"I should let you sleep." He said the words into her hair as his hand slid down to massage her neck.

"I like this."

"Now, don't take this the wrong way, but I think most women like cuddling."

"And it scares the crap out of most men."

"They're idiots, then, because having a naked woman, all warm and beautiful, crowded up against you is not a bad thing."

She smiled against his skin before placing a quick kiss on his chest. "I meant the talking and touching. The sense of intimacy."

He raked his hand through her hair in a hypnotic beat that compared to the simple joy of brushing hair. "I think what you said is probably a nicer way of saying what I did, but yeah."

She hated to break the mood now that the amusement had moved back into his voice. "Why do you hate Los Angeles?"

"Bad memories."

"I'm familiar with those."

His other hand swept over the arm across his chest. His fingers touched under her chin and lifted her face. "Your strength amazes me."

"I have to be honest here." She searched his face, ready

to pick up on any sign of disappointment. "I'm scared all the time."

"So?"

"Does that sound like a strong person to you?"

"It sounds smart. The world can be scary, and yours more so than most." He kissed her, his lips passing over hers just long enough to ignite the flame before he pulled back. "Strength isn't about never being afraid. It's about pushing through when you are."

"How did you get so smart?" She was joking, but the way his eyebrows pulled together, she guessed he took her seriously.

"The hard way." His fingers tightened in her hair. "I messed up and my partner died."

The announcement stunned her. She'd come to view him as invincible, as someone who never made a wrong move. Looking closer, she saw the pain fill his eyes and the self-hatred flatten his mouth.

"Jonas, I'm so sorry."

"It was the only time in my life I hesitated. I held back and the guy we were chasing got the shot off first. My partner bled out before help came."

"Tell me his name."

"Henry McCarthy. Dead at thirty-one." The words ripped out of him as if he said them every morning in the mirror.

She traced her finger over Jonas's lips. "We all carry guilt that we should let go."

He shook his head. "I deserve mine."

The words shot through her and landed in a place she tried so hard to bury for so long. To the spot she could never scrub clean. That small space where logic disappeared and the doubts ruled.

If she'd come home, she could have saved them. If she hadn't fought with her parents the night before, her dad might have left the house earlier or stayed out later and would still be alive today.

If Jonas had lifted his gun faster, Henry would be alive.

The nonsense rationale depended on a could-have-been. The berating thoughts didn't have any basis in reality, but she knew how the doubts could pulse and grow.

She wanted better for Jonas, at least for tonight.

She crawled up his body until she straddled him. Her hair cascaded over his chest as she balanced over him. "Let me help you forget."

He brushed her hair behind her ears. "Yes."

"I can wipe it all away. Replace the bad memories with good ones."

He pushed on her lower back until she flattened her body against his. "We'll keep trying until you do."

Chapter Seventeen

Jonas felt the unwanted heat from Rich's stare and ignored it and him. They sat across from each other at Jonas's dining-room table. Rich had showed up far too early with boxes in hand and the promise of still-warm doughnuts. Jonas would have appreciated the quick turnaround on the information and the sugary wake-up call if he had slept more than three hours the night before.

Not that he was complaining.

Thinking about Courtney and all they did while rolling across his mattress had him smiling. He could still smell her when he inhaled. Still taste her on his lips.

"Stop doing that," Rich mumbled.

"What's wrong with you?"

Rich threw down his pen and glared. "Your happiness is annoying as—"

Jonas held up a hand. "Okay, I get it."

Rich balanced his crossed arms behind his head. "It's just that things are quiet right now for me."

"Maybe if we worked this case you'd feel better." Jonas pointed to the paperwork spread out over every inch of the table.

If Rich picked up on the hint, he pedaled around it. "It's not as if there are a huge number of available women in Aberdeen."

"We're off track here." It wasn't like Rich to stray off work and go on a woman tangent, and Jonas wasn't ready to talk about Courtney or what happened last night or what could happen tomorrow. "I was saying I appreciate you showing up with breakfast."

Rich snorted. "Sure you were."

"I like doughnuts." Jonas held one up as proof.

"Yeah, your mood is about the food."

Jonas shoved a box into Rich's line of sight. "I can't hear you."

"I assume everything went well last night."

Was it written on his face or something? Jonas pushed the box off to the side again. "What did you say?"

Rich bit his lip but the smile escaped, anyway. "I'm talking safety-wise. You did have an attempted break-in here yesterday."

"I know."

Rich lowered his arms and folded them on the table in front of him. "Do you?"

The murders and other crimes never strayed far from Jonas's mind. Even after Courtney fell asleep last night, he lay there turning over all the facts, trying to find an answer.

Paul Eckert. Ron Stimpson. The man in the forest whom Walt still hadn't identified. It all traced back to Cade Willis. No matter what the reason or how the timing fell out, that was a long list of men searching for Courtney and involved in a decade-old crime the police considered closed.

Someone was willing to kill an FBI agent to keep secrets hidden, a move that guaranteed feds would be crawling all over this case any minute now. Once they figured out this wasn't about an agent killed on vacation, the questions would start and so would the press coverage. Jonas was trying to keep the lid on it until then. To stall and get some traction before he lost the lead.

The same someone who killed Eckert risked everything to make a run at Jonas's back door, and possibly hired the guy to kill Courtney in the forest and grab her at Stimpson's place.

The fire chief thought a gas leak might explain the apartment explosion, but Jonas didn't buy the coincidence. He didn't have to sort through the burned pieces to know the inspector would come to a different conclusion.

The path of death and destruction kept growing. That meant they were dealing with a person with nothing to lose. And that scared the hell out of Jonas.

But outward panic wouldn't solve anything. Neither would talking about his sex life. He wasn't that guy, anyway. Neither was Rich, but if his wide eyes meant anything he sure seemed interested in the details this time around.

"No problems with intruders last night," Jonas said. "Thanks for your concern about my well-being."

"The officer stationed outside your door filled me in on what happened here last night."

Jonas caught something in Rich's voice but ignored it. This likely fell into the category of things Jonas didn't want to know or dissect. "We were fine."

"From the stupid look on your face, I'd say more than fine."

"Don't."

"Hey." Rich held up his hands. "I'm not Walt. I'm all for you having some fun."

Another problem. "What's with Walt?"

"He's stepping into the role of your dad and worrying about things like whether you're having safe sex and dating the right woman, and don't change the subject."

Jonas blew out a long breath. "In case you can't tell, I'm not comfortable talking about Courtney like this."

"That's good to know."

Both men spun around at the sound of her voice. She stood in the kitchen doorway with her contacts back in and a coffee cup in her hands. A smile tugged on the corner of her mouth.

The jeans and sweater covered her body, but Jonas remembered everything. Long legs. Athletic but still-curvy body. Soft skin. Curious hands. Hot mouth.

Much more of this and he'd have to kick Rich out and not worry about the consequences. "Morning."

She nodded in the direction of Jonas's hand. "Have any more doughnuts?"

"You don't look like you've eaten one in…" Rich's gaze did a quick trip down her body and back again. "Well, ever."

"Do you want to die?" Jonas didn't bother to mumble the question.

"Don't let the waistline fool you. It's metabolism. I have the diet of a fifteen-year-old boy." She moved to the head of the table and rested her coffee on top of one of the closed boxes.

Jonas lifted the mug and put it on the table next to his. Last thing he needed was a complaint that he ruined evidence by spilling coffee all over it. "I bet other women love you."

Courtney frowned. "That reminds me. Can we check on Ellie today?"

Jonas wanted to kick his own butt for not thinking about performing an informal wellness check. Ellie had been at Courtney's house and discovered the break-in. The woman had shaken in her seat belt during the entire drive back to her place yesterday. She'd had a scare. She had to be worried and more than a little confused.

Rich sat up straighter. "Ellie Wise?"

"You know her?" Courtney's eyes widened as she asked.

"Sure, she owns the bookstore." Rich stared at both of them again. "What? I read."

Courtney laughed as she lifted the top off a box. "What's all this?"

"Wait." Jonas came up and out of his chair in a flash. His hand slapped against the lid, knocking it out of her hand. "No."

"Stop," Rich said at the same time.

Her gaze shot between them. "What's wrong with you two?"

"Nothing." Jonas tried to pull her away from the table. "I just can't have civilians touching case materials."

Rich wedged his body between her and the table. "It's a chain-of-custody issue."

She delivered on of those looks that said she thought they were idiots. "You're both lying."

"The boxes are on loan to us," Jonas said.

She put her hand on Rich's arm and he stepped aside. "This is the file on my dad's case." She traced her finger over the case number on the side of the box. "How did you get it?"

"I had it shipped in. Called in some favors and got it here fast." Rich returned to his seat and tried to drag the box across the tabletop with him.

She grabbed the edge and stopped him. "Why?"

Jonas stepped behind her. With as gentle a touch as possible, he pried her hands off the cardboard. "I don't know how to look into the murders and figure out who committed them without going through all of this stuff, page by horrible page."

She turned until she stood in the safe zone between his arms. Her finger slid across his jaw before her hand dropped. "Okay."

He continued to hold his breath. "We're good?"

"You believe me, so we're better than good."

The need to pull her close burned through him, but he

held on to his control. They had a witness. More important, Jonas knew he had to exercise some distance on this.

"I know you believe someone else did the crime, and that's good enough for me to double-check everything." And he wasn't playing. Separating the woman from the case grew harder each day.

Rich cleared his throat. "Me, too."

His voice killed the moment and for once Jonas was grateful for the interference.

She moved his arm and stepped away. When Jonas looked up again, she sat in his chair eating the last few bites of his doughnut.

She read through the notes he made on the yellow legal pad. "What are you expecting to find in all of this?"

"Motives for someone other than your dad. Mistakes in the investigations. Notes on other suspects." Jonas ticked off the list.

Courtney shot Rich a side glance. "Do you—"

"He filled me in." The lightness had left Rich's voice. The usual joking manner gave way to a tone both serious and caring. "I'm really sorry."

"Thanks."

Jonas didn't know when or how it happened, but she'd woven her spell around Rich, as well. He'd once eyed her with suspicion. Now, only a few days later, he accepted her in Jonas's house.

The realization filled him with pride and discomfort. Making room for her came too easy.

To get his mind off his runaway truck of a private life, he focused on the disaster in front of him. "We have a cold-case protocol that involves looking at the case with fresh eyes, no preconceived notions. We're going to use the system here."

Rich tapped his fingers on the top of the box. "That means everything."

"I don't see the problem," Courtney said, her confusion obvious in the lines around her eyes.

Jonas did. "I'll keep the crime-scene photos on a bulletin board in the extra bedroom upstairs. Stay out of there and—"

"There's no need to hide them." She put all her concentration into ripping the remaining doughnut into tiny pieces. "I've seen everything."

Rich glanced at Jonas then back to her. "How?"

She shrugged. "I once paid an investigator to gather information. I also pressured the police and raised a fuss until the police let me see some of the file. I borrowed the rest and made copies."

"Borrowed?"

"Do you really want to know?" Courtney shot Rich the *duh* look Jonas knew so well.

Rich put his hands over his ears. "I'm actually sorry I asked."

Jonas didn't find any part of the conversation funny. The idea of her studying the evidence punched a hole in his stomach. "There's a reason to keep the photos and some of the tougher stuff away from the victims' families."

She piled the doughnut crumbs on a napkin. "Which is?"

"To spare you."

An anger Jonas hadn't seen since that first day on the porch darkened her face. "My family was murdered and my father was blamed. There's nothing left to protect me from."

Jonas's festering frustration melted away. It was that simple.

She was right. She'd lived with it and let it run over every other part of her life. She knew what she could handle.

But that didn't mean he'd stop trying to protect her. "Just stay out of the bedroom."

A crushing quiet followed his grumbled response. The

energy sucked right out of the room. Tension thumped off every wall and thickened the air.

Finally Rich broke the stalemate. "Why aren't we doing this at the station?"

Jonas welcomed the return to safer ground. In his usual business life, people listened to him. Only Courtney pretended deafness to his orders. "Because someone pulled Stimpson off that door and knew to get to him before I could."

"You think there's a mole in the police force." Rich nodded as he said it.

Courtney frowned. "You do?"

Jonas wasn't ready to dissect that issue as part of an open conversation yet. "I think we handle this quietly for now."

"Who else knows about my past?" she asked.

"Walt, as soon as he gets here."

She made a face. "The guy who hates me."

"He doesn't…" Jonas looked to Rich for help, but his friend quickly lowered his head. Jonas scrambled to find the right words. When that failed, he went with the shortest sentence he could come up with: "Walt is worried."

"He thinks you rob Jonas's good judgment."

Now Rich speaks up. Jonas would thank him for the delayed response later. "Rich, that's enough."

"She's a smart woman, Jonas. She knows what's going on."

She winked at Rich. "You, I like."

"And me?" Jonas asked.

Her head dipped to the side and she flashed him a heated smile. "You're growing on me."

Chapter Eighteen

The ding of the doorbell kept Jonas from doing something stupid. Something like clearing the room and the table and her clothing.

"Expecting someone?" she asked.

"Your admirer, Walt. He has the video from the night Eckert was killed."

"The murderer was dumb enough to get caught on film?" Courtney asked Rich, as Jonas answered the door.

"Apparently."

Jonas traded welcomes with Walt and showed him into the dining room. He saw the older man's shoulders stiffen when he rounded the corner and Courtney came into view. The reaction struck Jonas as overblown. She was a victim and he treated her like the enemy.

Since he'd known Walt, and that encompassed most of his life, Jonas watched Walt protect and serve. He'd stuck by a sick wife debilitated by multiple sclerosis, refusing to throw away the first twenty-five years of their marriage to run from the end of it. When she died, Walt hibernated and mourned. He'd only ventured back into life when Jonas moved to town.

"Ms. Allen." Walt nodded in her general direction but didn't give her eye contact.

"Please, call me Courtney."

Jonas wasn't in the mood for stilted conversation, so he

pushed the topic where he wanted it to go. "What did you find?"

"We have our killer's face." Walt turned around the hand-held video camera and they all crowded around him. "Here he is."

The monitor was small and the video a bit grainy, thanks to the hospital equipment. Jonas watched the man flash a badge at Stimpson then push his way into Eckert's room. Short blond hair and a dark suit, and an age close to Jonas's own.

He never looked at the camera, but he didn't hide from it, either. Chances were he missed the equipment, which would have been easy since it was outside the regular security system. Jonas had his men plant this one at the nurses' station. Only a few people knew about its existence. Even Walt hadn't known until Jonas had asked him to retrieve it that morning.

Walt glanced around the circle. "Any idea who it is before I start running the image through our databases and call in the FBI for help?"

Courtney stepped back and leaned against the table. "Cade Willis."

"Who?" Rich asked.

Walt's face turned white. "Did you say Willis?"

She swallowed several times before answering. "His father killed mine."

Walt blinked. "Excuse me?"

They'd all stopped, frozen in their places. No one said anything as Rich rewound the video and watched it a second time.

Jonas knew he had to bring Walt up to speed. He was both a friend and sheriff. He needed all of the facts. Not only would it make them all safer, knowing about Courtney's past might ease whatever concerns the older man had brewing in his head about her.

But Jonas had to focus on the new information right now. "Are you sure that's him?"

"We've been circling each other for years. I have a file on him two inches thick upstairs." She hitched her thumb toward the second floor. "I don't have to see his face to know it's Cade Willis. I even have the walk memorized."

Walt still hadn't moved. "I don't understand what's going on."

"That's the other reason I asked you to come over." Jonas laid his hand on top of the closest box. "This is the case file relating to the murders of Courtney's family."

"Family?"

"Parents and two sisters." She delivered the information without any emotion.

Her detachment sent a warning signal across Jonas's nerves. He looked at the file and his stomach hollowed out. The more she talked about it, the more it sounded as if she was reading a grocery list.

"When?" Walt asked.

"Ten years ago."

"I still don't understand what that has to do with what's happening now."

Rich asked the unspoken question that played in Jonas's brain day and night. If Jonas could find that piece, he could unravel the entire mess.

"I was digging around in the evidence, asking questions and trying to get someone to listen to me about Cade's father. To review everything again and point a new investigation in his direction," Courtney said. "I'm guessing something I found scared someone."

Walt sat down hard on one of the chairs. "What is happening here?"

"I got the fake call to check on her, went over there and set off a chase. We've been running ever since we met up with that guy in the forest." Jonas hated his part in this. He didn't regret meeting her. Even now he looked at her and saw something special, but he helped set it all in motion.

The confusion left Walt's eyes. "The easiest answer is for you to leave."

Rich sighed. "Walt, that's out of line."

Courtney's face flushed a deep red. If she held on to the back of the chair any tighter, she'd snap the wood in half. "I happen to live here, in this town, and I'm not letting anyone push me out. I refuse to be a victim, but I'm not the bad guy here, either."

Jonas clapped his hands to get their attention. The crack had them all looking in his direction. "Fighting and turning on each other aren't going to get this job done. We have to track down Cade and ask him some questions. One wrong answer and I'll arrest him."

"One thing is certain. Contacting the FBI isn't the right way to go since Cade *is* FBI. He went to law school and right into the agency for training." Her mouth flattened the longer she talked. "He's been working his way up ever since. One of these days he'll probably run the place and use his position to publicly condemn my father and insist the case is completely closed."

"Isn't it already?" Rich looked to Jonas. "I mean technically?"

"The police determined my father did it and stopped looking elsewhere," she said. "That's not closed in my mind."

Walt stared at his hands. Flipped them over and studied the nails then the palms. "I talked with him."

"Who?" Jonas asked.

"That's the name of the guy I called at the FBI when I hit Redial on Eckert's phone."

Rich was the first to say anything. "Interesting."

"Willis is the person who picked up. There were other calls. I made a list of names." Walt slipped a piece of paper out of his chest pocket and handed it to Jonas. "Here."

"I can check the others," Rich said.

Walt stood up and pointed at Jonas. "Can I talk with you for a second?"

Jonas dreaded another man-to-man discussion, but he passed the paper to Rich and followed Walt. "Sure."

They only made it as far as the front porch before Walt unloaded. "I know you're not going to listen to my warnings about Courtney."

"No, I'm not." Jonas hoped that would end the conversation but he was rarely that lucky these days.

"You're too close to this and you know it."

Jonas stared across the lawn. The sun beamed down on the grass, but the chill hadn't left the air. Being this close to the water meant freak rainstorms and rare hot spells. The weather suited the mood hovering over Jonas since he moved there.

Today, racing white clouds or not, he welcomed the bright blue sky. "She's under my protection, like everyone else in Aberdeen."

"You sleeping with them, too?"

Something inside Jonas deflated. A man didn't have any privacy in a small town. "How did you—"

"The way you put your body in front of hers. The way you look at her." Walt rubbed a hand over his head. "Damn, Jonas. What are you thinking?"

"We're not talking about this."

"Let me take her. I can get her out of Aberdeen and hide her in another town until we catch this Willis guy."

The pleading in Walt's voice chipped away at Jonas's resolve. Walt thought he knew the right thing and was trying to act on it. Jonas appreciated it. Appreciated everything the man had ever done for him, including stepping in as a mentor when Jonas's dad died.

Jonas had to call up the image of Courtney's face to stay on track. His loyalty to Walt tugged at him, but Jonas pushed it out. He'd made her a promise and issued a vow.

"She stays with me." He said the words without any doubts or regrets.

Walt swore as he kicked at a loose floorboard on the porch. "Then at least promise me that if this gets worse you'll call me to pick her up. I may not think your relationship is a good idea for you, but I can keep her safe."

"I know."

"The best way to do that might be to take her out of Aberdeen, if only for a few days."

Walt could handle the job. There was no one Jonas trusted with Courtney's safety more than Walt and Rich. "I appreciate that."

"But you're still saying no."

Jonas couldn't imagine a time when he wouldn't say no, but he didn't share that piece. "If I can't handle it, I'll call."

Chapter Nineteen

Later that afternoon Courtney sat in Jonas's car and stared across the highway at the one-story motel on the other side. Unexpected rain in the form of a fine mist greeted them the second they slowed to a stop alongside the gas station. Drops spread over the windows, blurring her view of the run-down building.

She tapped her fingernails against the gearshift as she scanned the area. The place looked abandoned. It needed a paint job and a better location. The outskirts of Aberdeen, which offered only the shelves of junk food from the gas station for supplies, didn't exactly say "tourist destination" to her.

Then again, neither did Aberdeen. The area, with its mountains on one side and water on the other, had a strikingly beautiful, open feel to it, but the town fell into the hidden-gem category. The locals liked the quiet and didn't use big marketing campaigns to invite outsiders in. The insular nature of the town was one of the reasons she'd picked it.

A figure dressed in dark pants with a windbreaker pulled tight over his head slipped out of the motel-management office. After waiting for a truck to pass, he jogged across the street toward where she sat in the car. She didn't panic because nothing about this particular man scared her.

Jonas opened the door, bringing a wave of damp air with

him. He slammed the door to the whistling wind and blew on his hands. "Man, the storm blew in out of nowhere."

"Welcome to Oregon."

"I don't think I'll ever get used to the radical changes in weather." He shook his head and water drops sprinkled over the seat. They beaded on his jacket and clung to the ends of his hair.

She brushed her fingers through the back near his neck. The intimate gesture was as natural as breathing. Completely inappropriate for a stakeout, of course. They weren't making out in the backseat of a car. They were hunting for clues.

When she pulled her hand back, he moved his head closer again. "That feels good."

"I still think you should be in the hospital."

"The scan said no concussion."

She rolled her eyes. "Because that's the test for getting right back on the job. Whether or not your skull is cracked."

"It actually is." He turned his head and shot her one of those sexy smiles.

She wanted to be immune but she wasn't. "I give up arguing with you about this."

"Good."

"For now. I'll be ready to call for an ambulance just in case." Her gaze traveled back to the motel. "Any trouble?"

"No. The manager recognized Cade from the tape. He's using another name, of course."

"Nothing suspicious about that."

"He's in room number three. Dead center." Jonas rubbed his hands together.

"The car is on the far end." She recognized it from the hospital tape.

They'd replayed both tapes, the official one from the hospital and Jonas's hidden one, several times that morning. While they crowded around the small screen, they watched

Cade walk in and out of Eckert's room as if nothing out of the ordinary happened. Forget the fact a man lay dying on the floor. Cade killed without even changing his facial expression.

Like father, like son.

Jonas made them take the video replay back even further. He matched Cade's entrance into the hospital with the section of the security tape that showed Cade pulling his rental car into the lot then walking across the pavement. Piecing together different time stamps, they could track his every step into the building.

From there, Jonas had clicked and refocused and zoomed in until he caught part of the license plate. One of his officers tracked down the rest, calling the rental-car companies near Aberdeen, and found the exact car that led them here.

The easy trail of police work impressed her. Nothing showy, just solid investigative work. They all stuck with it until they connected the dots.

Cade added to the chain by keeping some of his tracks clear. He'd paid cash for the car but provided a copy of his driver's license. The evidence directed them right here.

Jonas insisted it had been too easy.

"Your only job is to give me a positive identification," he said in a voice low and dark.

That quickly, the man morphed back into the cop. She understood it, but she didn't always like the harsh change. Just when his mood lured her in, he started issuing orders.

And he wondered why she rarely obeyed.

She dropped her hand back on her lap. "I thought I already did that when I looked at the video."

Jonas folded his hand over hers and dragged it to his thigh. "You talked about knowing a guy's body type and walk."

"Yeah."

"That's a little thin, don't you think?"

Typical male reaction. They had no idea what facts a woman could pick up from the slightest things. Her training in illustration helped, but all women had the gift. Where men could be clueless, women thrived on intuition.

"I'd know you from the way you walk. You could be headed in the opposite direction wearing a coat, and I'd pick you out," she said.

"You do have a bit more personal experience with my body."

Her cheeks flared with heat. "Are you trying to change the subject?"

"Just trying to get some circulation back into my leg."

She followed his gaze and saw how her nails were digging into his dark jeans. "Sorry."

"I prefer pleasure to pain."

"I'm happy to hear that."

Jonas put a hand on the wheel and leaned in. "There aren't any lights."

He switched topics on a breath and she rushed to catch up. "What?"

"It's dark out, thanks to the rain. His curtains are drawn. I don't even see the reflection of the television."

Jonas turned over the car's engine. A blast of heat blew across her feet. After two swipes of the windshield wipers the view of the motel cleared. Only one of the windows other than the management office had a light.

"How many people are staying there?" she asked, sure Jonas would have tracked that information down.

"Four."

She snuck a peek at Cade's rental again. Rain ran down the windows and dripped into the parking space below, suggesting it hadn't moved in some time. "Maybe he's sleeping."

"Maybe he snuck out."

She couldn't swallow over the sudden lump in her throat. "You think he knows we're over here?"

"He's been trained. His partner is dead. That makes the walls close in on a guy." Jonas's hand flexed on the wheel. "Trust me."

"But—"

"We're going in closer." Jonas put the car in gear.

They glided out of their hiding place to the edge of the road. Two cars passed, spraying water in every direction. When the short spurt of traffic cleared, Jonas drove across the road. Gravel crunched under the tires as he came to a stop three spaces down from Cade's rental car.

The lump stopped her breath and the churning in her stomach threatened to double her over. "This guy is a killer."

"So?"

Now that the confrontation time had come, her brain cried for her to run. Coming face-to-face with the man determined to ruin her father's memory made her head spin. She expected to feel a rush of power. Instead, her muscles melted to liquid.

"I don't think we should push him." Her teeth chattered hard enough for her to hear the clicking. "I know I tend to say this a lot, but you should call for backup."

"For what?"

"What?"

"I don't have any evidence or probable cause."

"Is that the point?"

Jonas finally focused on her instead of the motel. His gaze roamed all over her, stopping at her foot thumping against the floor. "What's wrong with you?"

"This is a mistake."

Before she could put an explanation together in her head, her door whipped open and she fell backward. Strong hands pulled her out of the car and into the rain. She would have fallen, but an arm banded tight around her waist and set her upright.

"Why are you following me?" Cold metal pressed against her temple.

She couldn't see her attacker, but she knew. Cade Willis had come to finish the work his father started.

Instead of jumping out of the car, Jonas opened the door nice and slow. The tip of his gun appeared over the top of the car first. Then he stood up, his eyes filled with a killing fury as the rain pounded down on him.

He walked around to the front with his jaw fixed and his gun aimed behind her. He didn't bother to wipe the water from his face. His expression said it all. He would shoot and not think twice. Cade started the death dance and Jonas was prepared to end it.

He stopped and stiffened his stance. "Drop it, Willis."

"I'm FBI." The anger in Cade's voice matched the eerie calm in Jonas's.

"I don't care."

"You don't want the feds coming down on your town."

"What makes you think you're going to live to tell anyone where you are?"

A tremor ran through Cade and rumbled against her. He talked tough and didn't back down, but Jonas affected him. She didn't know how he couldn't. Tall and dressed in black, Jonas wore the look of an avenging angel.

"Put the gun down and I'll let her go." Cade yelled the order in her ear.

She flinched and ducked her head away from him. Quickly, Jonas's fingers moved. She could see him wrestle with the idea of killing Cade on the spot, no chances. Part of her wanted the man dead, but she'd settle for having him answer some questions then disappear forever.

Even through the waves of nausea and blinding fear, she

wanted the truth. She stood close enough that his hot breath tickled against her neck. If she could turn around and smack him, keep hitting until he admitted his father's sins, she would.

But he had her in a tight hold. The rain had soaked her shirt. The sound of the rushing water and thunder in the distance echoed in her ears. Cars whizzed by, but her entire world focused on Jonas's hands on that weapon.

Jonas's gaze never left Cade's face. "Let her go and I won't shoot you in the head."

"This isn't a negotiation. I'm calling the shots."

Jonas kept walking. He was at the front edge of the car closest to them now, only a few feet away now. "Not sure how well you did in sharpshooting class at the agency, but I was considered an expert in the army."

Cade barked out a shaky laugh. "We can both hit at this distance."

"But I'm willing to die for her. Are you?"

Her heart flipped at Jonas's admission. Deep inside, in that part of her she'd closed off and abandoned, she knew he was telling the truth. This wasn't a game to him.

She closed her eyes and prayed Cade would give in. She dug her fingernails into his arm. "Listen to Jonas."

Cade ignored her, didn't even flinch. "You wouldn't risk her life, Porter."

"I won't hesitate to put you down like the sick animal you are. Wouldn't be the first time the job called for it. Working the streets of Los Angeles taught me that."

"We're in Oregon now, Deputy."

"And I can do all of those things I promised without touching her." A knowing calm washed over Jonas. "Just test me."

After a second of hesitation, the weight around her middle

eased. She didn't wait. She bolted to Jonas's side and slipped her body half behind his.

She could see Cade now. The photos in her file didn't highlight his size. He'd gone from a skinny college kid screaming at her in the courthouse to a man in a Kevlar vest with dark patches under his eyes.

"What do you want from me?" The question ripped out of her, the words tumbling out before she could stop them.

"The truth."

Jonas didn't lower his gun or relax his muscles. She knew because she had a death grip on the back of his shirt. Every part of him was on high alert.

"What the hell does that mean?" he asked. "Answer her question."

"She won't let it drop, won't accept what her father did. She keeps on going and accusing my dad. She harasses the cops and insists on meetings with the prosecutors."

"How dare you—"

"You've made my life hell." Cade's words thundered over the pounding rain.

"I did what I had to do. And I don't regret it."

"My father is dead because of you." Cade's anguished cry drowned out the sounds of the cars honking as they passed.

The noise, so primal and lost, battered against her wall of hatred. She recognized the mind-numbing pain because she'd heard it in her own voice. The mouth twisted with rage and the hands clenched as if to fight off the thoughts that constantly assailed him. She'd lived through it all.

To keep strong, she let her mind flood with the memories of the shocking crime-scene photos. Blood splashed everywhere. Her sister hunted down and shot in the back of the head in her girlie-pink bedroom.

Then there was the fear that had wrapped around her

every day, everything Courtney did since then, as she waited for her family's killer to come and get her, too. She'd slept in her closet for weeks. She moved across the country to hide while she investigated.

She lost everything—her family, her security and her future.

From behind the safety of Jonas's shoulders, she shouted all that built-up rage at Cade, letting it spew and engulf her. "Your father killed my family. He tried before and failed to hurt a woman, but he succeeded with the people I loved."

The gun shook in Cade's hands. "That's not true. That other woman lied. My father never touched her."

The shout caught in her throat let go. "Wake up, Cade."

Cade tapped the side of his gun against his chest. "I was there. I saw that woman rip my family apart with her lies and all because my father sued her. Her claims were discredited and the prosecutor refused to file charges."

"Your dad got lucky that time. Once he got away with it, he had the taste." And her family paid the price for that series of poor decisions.

"No." Cade shook his head and mumbled as if lost in his own thoughts. "My dad liked your family. Your father gave him a chance."

"And look what happened."

"Your father killed them all and you wouldn't accept it."

"No." She covered her ears. "No. It was Tad Willis. He was there that day and tried to cover it up. The police found his fingerprints in the house."

"He feared he'd be blamed, so he lied at first. He'd used a bathroom and left while everyone was still alive and fine. How could he make people believe that?"

Cade had an answer for everything. He said the facts as if he believed them.

"Then why did he kill himself?" The roaring in her ears blinked off, replaced with a sudden, shocking silence. "Why would an innocent man do that?"

"Because he couldn't take it." Cade shook his gun at her as his face crumbled.

Jonas shifted his weight until his body blocked her view of Cade. "And you followed your father's lead and came here and killed Paul Eckert. Did he get in your way or were you afraid he'd uncover your past?"

Cade's shoulders fell as his mouth dropped open. "What?"

In the split second when Cade's gun wavered, Jonas sprang into action. She screamed his name as he lunged over the front edge of the car and hit Cade square in the chest. The gun skittered across the pavement and under Cade's car as the men went down.

They rolled across the wet pavement, rain on them as they punched and kicked. Cade landed a shot to Jonas's jaw that sent his head flying back.

"Jonas!" She turned and called out to the manager for help but the door never opened. Two men stood across the street at the station but didn't come over.

They were on their own.

She stopped watching the fight long enough to search the ground for one of the guns. A flash of metal by her feet had her bending down and picking it up. Even in the cold, the metal pressed warm against her skin.

When she looked up again, arms and legs flailed. She saw Cade's back then Jonas's stomach. They switched positions as they grunted and their clothing rustled. Water poured on them in a steady, unforgiving flow. Their elbows splashed in the deep puddles of the pockmarked lot.

The heavy weapon weighed down her arms as she followed the men's movements. She wanted to shoot a warning shot but worried she'd distract Jonas or hit a bystander. Shooting into the pile risked killing Jonas, and the thought of that made her stomach heave.

With a roaring shout, Jonas wrestled Cade to his back. Cade reared up, lifting his body off the ground, but Jonas shoved him back down again. From that position, with his hands on Cade's shoulders, Jonas smacked Cade's head against the pavement.

Cade turned and avoided most of the blow. He kicked out and bucked. But when Jonas leaned down and pressed an elbow into Cade's throat, the man stopped squirming. He looked up at Jonas with eyes glazed with fear as a choke strangled out of him.

Both men panted. Jonas's chest rose as he pushed out his words. "I'm going to kill you now."

She heard the comment and reached for Jonas. She tugged on his shoulders but it would have been easier to move a building. "No, he needs to pay for Eckert's death."

Cade coughed and sputtered. It took three tries for him to get the words out. "I didn't do it."

Jonas used his weight to press Cade even deeper into the pavement. "We have it on tape."

Cade put his hands on Jonas's arm. "He was my friend."

"As if you know what that means."

"He was alive."

"When?"

"When I left the room." Frantic now, his eyes darting from side to side, Cade looked at Courtney. "Ask the guard."

"He's dead." Jonas delivered the news as he stumbled to his feet, half-bent over and wheezing every few breaths.

Before she could react, he grabbed the gun out of her hands and aimed it at Cade's still form. "So is the guy you sent to kill Courtney earlier. I killed him and left him in the forest."

Cade's forehead wrinkled as his hands dropped to his sides against the hard ground. "Who are you talking about?"

The manager chose that moment to come outside. He shouted from the safety of his office. "I've called the police."

"I *am* the police," Jonas yelled back. Then he looked at Cade again. "Who else did you send after her? How many more are coming?"

Cade's chest rose on harsh breaths. "No one. Paul wasn't supposed to get hurt. I thought…"

Jonas lowered the gun, but only slightly. "What?"

"You killed Paul to protect her." Cade closed his eyes. When he opened them again, some of the daze had disappeared.

"Why would I do that?" Jonas asked.

"I don't know." Cade shook his head against the ground. "That's why I watched you when you drove up and sat across the street. I waited for you to drive over here to make a move and when you did—"

"You grabbed me." Courtney didn't want Cade's story to make sense. She wanted to keep him in the hatred column and write off everything he said as a lie to cover his father's murders. But as he talked, she felt their twisted connection over that horrible day.

Cade wiped the water from his face and the rain pelted him again. "I only came here to scare her."

"Congratulations," she mumbled.

"I have to get you to stop. My family has paid enough for your lies," he whispered.

Sirens wailed as flashing lights appeared over the slight hill down the road. Jonas wiped blood from the corner of his mouth. "You're going to jail."

But Cade wasn't listening. "If you didn't kill Paul, who did?"

Jonas glanced at her. "And why?"

Courtney wondered the same thing.

Chapter Twenty

Ellie came around the counter when the bell above her shop's front door dinged. "Can I help you?"

Kurt waved her off as he secretly locked the door and slipped into the high stacks lined with books. "Just looking."

She smiled at him as she returned to her stool by the cash register. "Enjoy."

He intended to savor but probably wouldn't enjoy. He'd never expected to start down this road. He'd been trying to save his family all those years ago. Allen had threatened to shut the partnership down over a simple bookkeeping issue. He wanted out, which meant refunding his investment and stopping contracts in midbid.

Kurt would have paid back the loan as soon as the money rolled in. Not taking an advance, limiting his draw to the bare minimum, had put his family's future at risk. But losing the partnership would have meant bankruptcy and likely the end of his marriage.

Allen wouldn't listen to reason or give him time, so Kurt didn't have a choice. If he got rid of Allen, the business would come to him. Taking out Allen's family ensured there wouldn't be any lengthy legal battles or annoying questions. Allen had to go out and take the blame, then Kurt could step in as the grieving partner.

And it all would have worked, all would have ended, if

Courtney had just shut up and gotten a life. Her being alive when she should have been dead was a huge problem and cost Kurt millions. Her playing amateur detective was a nightmare that could cost him his freedom.

For years she'd pushed and he'd begged her to move on. More than once she went to the police and he walked in behind her to clean up the mess and drop hints about her competency.

Then in an email a month ago she'd mentioned getting her dad's old business boxes, and Kurt knew he couldn't wait. The final Peters daughter needed to meet her end. She'd never been the good one, anyway. She was the artsy one. The waste.

All it had taken was a well-placed rumor about Courtney going after Cade's father again and getting the press to help her clear her father's name this time around. Kurt had tracked her down through their infrequent emails and made sure Cade had the information to go after her on his own.

It was the perfect ending. The son of the "real" killer, driven mad and desperate, would finish his father's most horrid work.

But bringing Courtney and Cade together proved more difficult than Kurt anticipated. Which led him to this bookstore. He glanced over at the shop owner. Thirty and divorced, she was the only friend of Courtney's that Kurt could find. Ellie was his last hope. He hoped Courtney's loyalty to her friend would lure her away from the deputy.

Kurt had seen what Porter did to the first man Kurt sent to grab Courtney. Thanks to back channels and cash payments, nothing could trace the dead man back to Kurt, but the death was a nuisance.

All Porter had to do that first time was make contact so Courtney would know to be afraid and try to run. Kurt's man had been ready to grab her, but no one had expected the deputy to hover, let alone run after her into the forest and shoot.

With Porter around, the plan would shudder to a halt. Kurt understood that now. It was either dispose of Porter, which would only raise questions and risk alienating Kurt's paid-for police help, or separate the deputy from Courtney and handle it that way. Kurt chose the latter.

And it had to happen fast. He'd killed the FBI agent to bring the authorities running and start the unraveling of Cade's careful world. Kurt had set up the tape to make sure Cade was implicated. That meant it was time to finish the job and get back home to work.

Kurt dragged his finger along the spines of a group of hardcover books lined on the shelves. "This is an impressive collection."

He didn't read the titles because he didn't care. He only picked them because they sat on the shelf closest to the woman he needed. Ellie.

"Are you searching for something special?" she asked.

"Definitely."

"If you have the title, I can look it up. If it's not here, I can order it." She clicked on her keyboard and left her hands poised, ready to type in whatever he said.

"I don't live around here."

She dropped her hands but her smile remained. "Are you on vacation?"

"A business trip."

"It's always nice to have something to read while you're away from home. We have commercial fiction and literary fiction." She pointed at different aisles as she spoke. "Do you have a preference?"

He'd had about enough with the walk through the make-shift library. Anyone could come in, and he wanted to take advantage of a break in the rain while he had the chance

Why anyone would ever choose to live in a water-drenched area like this was a mystery to him.

Ellie slid off her seat and walked around to stand next to him. "I can show you whatever you need."

"I'd like you to get Courtney to come here. Now."

Ellie's smile faltered. "What?"

"Your friend Courtney." Kurt grabbed Ellie's arm in a tight grip to keep her from running. "Her real name is Ann Peters, but I don't really care what she calls herself. I just need to talk with her."

"I don't understand."

He dragged Ellie to the opposite side of the counter. She dug in her heels. When she started to scream, he slapped a hand over her mouth and pulled her into the back office. The police station was not far away, and the last thing he needed was for some Good Samaritan with a gun to come running.

"Your dear friend is being difficult." He whispered the words against the woman's hair as he rounded her desk. Ellie trembled and winced at each syllable as he spoke.

"You could just call her." Ellie stuttered over the comment.

Ah, but that's not the plan. "No, but you will."

"You're not making any sense."

"Maybe this would help." He shoved her into her chair and took out his gun.

All the color drained from the woman's already pale face. Amazing how a weapon could change the conversation. Get it back on track.

"What are you doing with that?" she asked.

"I need you to tell Courtney to come here. Alone." He picked up the receiver and held it in front of Ellie's face.

"I don't—"

Kurt grabbed Ellie's purse off the edge of her desk and

dug around for her cell phone. He dumped that on the desk, too. Between a call and a test, Ellie would get the job done.

Or she better. "I am not in the mood to deal with the deputy police chief. He needs to stay away. Tell Courtney to come alone."

Ellie shook her head, sending her blond hair swinging. "He won't leave her side."

"Then you better be convincing. Make Courtney think you'll die if she doesn't slip away and get here." Kurt inched forward until the gun touched the woman's forehead. "Because, Ellie, you will."

JONAS WATCHED CADE put his wallet and gun on the desk for the inventory clerk to tag. They were at the police station. Jonas had done everything he could to intimidate the other man on the drive over. Nothing really worked, since Cade hadn't said a word or even looked up since Jonas walked him in the building.

Neither had Courtney. Even now, she sat in Jonas's big desk chair and stared straight ahead.

Rich joined Jonas in the doorway to his office, and after a quick glance in Courtney's direction, joined in watching Cade. "She okay?"

"No." Jonas wondered if she would ever be okay.

How could a person live through everything she had and come out the other side? She'd fostered her hatred for Cade, and when faced with the moment of victory, she'd looked as confused and panicked as a little kid lost in a department store.

Rich crossed his arms over his chest. "What do you think about this Willis character?"

The man in question mumbled answers to whatever questions he was being asked. He nodded and shuffled his feet.

His wet shirt hung untucked, as if he had just come through a fight, which he had.

Hardly the actions of a trained assassin out for a fresh kill. Cade struck Jonas more like a lost male version of Courtney.

"Courtney hates him," he said.

"You know that's not what I'm asking."

"His face when I mentioned Eckert…" Jonas shook his head and closed his eyes when the small shake sent pain bouncing around in there. "I don't think it was guilt. The accusation he killed his partner shook him, as if he was out there trying to find the murderer."

"So Willis really came here just to scare the crap out of Courtney and ended up getting his friend killed?" Rich whistled. "Try living with that."

Jonas had. Every single day since he left his last job he struggled with the crushing regret.

He'd shot a kid during a drug bust and then had to defend his actions when the kid's gangbanger friend and vocal family insisted Jonas pulled first. As if dealing with the death of a kid at his hands wasn't bad enough, he had to handle the aftermath. The fallout included a suspension and mandatory check-ins with an office shrink. The newspaper stories detailing the abuses of the Los Angeles Division of the DEA and its rogue officer—him—came later.

Not one word of the vile story was true, but the damage had been done. Jonas lost pay and the respect of his team. The entire division had to undergo special training. New regulations came down requiring more warnings before a shooting. The new protocol for delayed engagement put the agents at risk.

Basically, the administrative folks did everything they could think of to tie the hands of the people in the field. And everyone blamed Jonas. Everyone except Henry.

The case took a toll, wore Jonas down physically and mentally. His refusal to take medicine earned him an extended suspension. When he finally returned to the job things went okay for a while.

His boss would later call the disaster the result of a loss of self-confidence. Jonas called it a fast track to Henry's death. Out on a call, Henry waited to pull a gun. So did Jonas. But by the time the weapons came out Henry was on the ground and his killers were off and running.

Henry McCarthy, dead at thirty-one.

That's how the newspaper article started. The sentence was seared into Jonas's brain.

Jonas looked at Cade's slumped shoulders. Jonas tried to block out the heartbreak that had pounded off of Cade when he stood in the parking lot and talked about his father. Jonas tried to imagine how far he would go to clear his father's name. He'd do anything for the man who raised him and died before he witnessed Jonas's shame.

"Cade is as sure of his father's innocence as Courtney is of her father's," Jonas said.

"What do you think?" Rich asked.

"I'm wondering if they're both victims." Jonas knew she hated the word, but it fit here. Two families destroyed by a horrible act, spending years pointing fingers at each other instead of healing. "Their focus on each other could have let the person really responsible slip under the radar."

Rich exhaled. "You know what that means, right?"

"That another killer is loose in Aberdeen." Jonas glanced at Rich's fixed jaw. "We've both known that for a half hour and have been trying not to say it."

"I wanted it to be Willis so we could wrap the case up and end it."

"Me, too."

Rich kept his focus on Cade. "It's pretty hard to fathom all that death so close to a place many think makes Mayberry look a little loose."

"Let him go." Courtney's firm voice shot out of the back of the office.

Both Rich and Jonas turned around at the same time. She hadn't gotten up. Hadn't moved even an inch, as far as Jonas could tell. Her hands remained folded on top of his desk and her back stayed straight.

She was on the verge of falling apart. Under all that strength, she shook and trembled. Jonas never would have noticed it before. He saw it now. The determination hid a lifetime of pain. The attitude covered all the insecurities.

"He assaulted an officer." That was the charge Jonas put on the sheet. It would stick. Witnesses across the street and the motel manager saw Cade drag Courtney out of the car, saw it all unfold.

Her eyes finally focused. For the first time in what felt like forever, she stared at Jonas instead of looking through him. "Cade had it all figured out in his mind. You killed Eckert. Cade thought you were trying to kill him like you did his partner. It was self-defense."

Rich scoffed. "That's bull—"

"Cade was out of line and deserves a takedown. Rogue agents with a badge don't serve anyone." Jonas struggled to keep his voice calm. She didn't need any more drama today.

"Yeah." She pushed out of the seat and walked across the room. Even her footsteps seemed unsure and uneven. "But it was instinct."

Jonas snorted. "I'm not ready to forgive."

"You think *I* am? I still don't understand what's going on." Her wide eyes mirrored the confusion in her voice.

"Do you think he's the one who's trying to kill you?" Rich asked.

"No."

Her answer surprised Jonas. "Why?"

"He carries a gun and a badge and could have walked right up to my door and taken me away without ever involving you. So few people know me here that it would have taken days, maybe weeks, for anyone to notice I was gone. By then I would have been dead." She sighed as if the weight of the world had been dropped on her shoulders. "No, this is something deeper."

"The real killer?" Rich separated each word with a pause.

She let out a harsh laugh. "I don't even know how to answer that."

Jonas's heart ripped in two over the sight of this beautiful, amazing woman brought to her knees. "Courtney—"

"I was so sure Tad Willis killed them all." She looked up at Jonas, her eyes clouded with tears. "What if I was wrong?"

He cupped her cheek. "And what if he read his dad all wrong? Maybe his dad did it."

"And Cade is not exactly innocent in this. He wanted to scare you, to break you," Rich said.

Jonas was deathly afraid Cade had succeeded.

She turned her head and pressed a kiss in Jonas's open palm. "I just want to go home and go to sleep."

Her words kicked him right in the gut, each syllable a crack against his ribs. "I don't think your house is safe."

"I mean your place." She dropped Jonas's hand and walked back into his office. "Let Cade go while I get my stuff."

Rich watched her. "That's a fine woman right there."

Jonas wasn't sure how he felt about the house thing, but he sure didn't hate it. The idea of waking up with her, holding her, settled inside him on a wave on contentment. "Yeah, tell me about it."

If she could make this bold move, he could answer with one of his own. He stepped up to the counter. They were about the same height but he seemed to loom over Cade. The man shrank as he stood.

Jonas signaled to the man behind the desk. "Give Agent Willis his property back."

The officer frowned. "Sir?"

For the first time since they walked in the door, the other man looked up. Jonas could feel the heat of Cade's stare. "Ms. Allen has decided not to press charges. I'm holding off…for now."

Cade finally faced Jonas. "Why?"

"What matters is what I'm about to tell you." Jonas leaned against the counter and pitched his voice low. He didn't need an audience for this. Some conversation had to be handled man-to-man. "You finish whatever business you have here over the Eckert murder, then you leave. You don't come near Courtney ever again. You don't talk with her or contact her. Hell, I don't want you thinking about her."

Something that looked like hope moved in Cade's green eyes. "And?"

"You do that and manage to clean your reputation over the Eckert murder and him being in town, and I'll leave you alone. You can have your life back, but you're on your own on your part in getting Eckert to come to Aberdeen. You get to explain that to your people." Jonas exhaled. "But I'll keep my mouth shut."

"I appreciate that."

"But you bother her in any way, or have anyone else do it by tracking her down or following her, and criminal charges will be the least of your problems."

"You."

"Yeah, me." Jonas leaned in closer. "Look, I don't know the answer about the murders, but I'm thinking someone is setting you both up. You investigate somewhere else, and away from her, and I'll stay out of your business."

Cade nodded. "Why are you letting me go now?"

"It was her, not me." Jonas slipped the arrest paperwork off the desk and crumpled it in a ball. "She's giving you a chance. I'd take it."

Cade stared at Jonas in a visual showdown that quickly fizzled. He grabbed his property and turned around. "I didn't send any of those men except Eckert."

"Meaning?"

"I'm not a killer."

"So you keep saying."

"There's someone else after her, and I'm thinking that person could clear my dad."

Jonas's stomach turned over at the thought. He could fight a foe he could see. This mystery attacker added layers Jonas didn't need. "That's for me to worry about. You get lost."

Chapter Twenty-One

After all that had happened, Courtney's nerves went numb. She couldn't feel anything. Her muscles worked, but her arms and legs weighed more than she could lift. Even walking hurt. And her brain was set to permanent misfire.

She didn't understand how she could put her life back together again or where to turn. All she knew was that she wasn't ready to leave Jonas's side. Good news was that he didn't seem inclined to push her away.

"Courtney?" He called out from the dining room. "Everything okay in there?"

"Sure."

"You can turn on the television."

She didn't have the strength or the interest to search for the remote. Sitting sucked up all her energy. She hovered at the point of having to remind her lungs to breathe.

They'd been home from the station, from Jonas's latest beating on her behalf, for less than an hour and already he was back to work. He had the files spread out on the table and the boxes opened. Where the burst of energy came from, she'd never know.

Rich had promised to check on Ellie, then he would be by to assist. That allowed Courtney time to concentrate very hard on doing nothing.

She lay curled up on the couch with a blanket pulled up

over her feet and ran her fingers through her still-damp hair. The rhythmic pull allowed her to get lost in random thoughts. She'd changed into dry clothes, but her body refused to get warm.

She knew she should stand up and walk into the dining room and help. She'd memorized every paper about the case that she could get her hands on over the past ten years. There could be new information in the boxes. Combining the facts in her head with whatever new information waited in those files could resolve everything.

But her brain needed rest. She wanted to go one hour, one minute even, without thinking about Cade Willis or her family or anything related to murder and attacks.

If she closed her eyes she saw Cade's mental implosion in the parking lot. If she opened them, she saw her father's face pleading with her to clear his name.

Even without those competing images, the idea of hiding in her thoughts proved impossible. A killer still lurked and no one in Aberdeen was safe until they figured out the person's identity and stopped him.

"Courtney?" She heard Jonas's chair scrape against the floor as he got up. Then his hands touched her shoulders and rubbed in a gentle massage. "Where are you? Your body is here but I'm not reaching the rest of you."

"I'm just distracted."

Jonas balanced his leg on the armrest behind her. "If you need to do some work, we can set up a place for your illustration. I won't pretend to know what you need, but I can figure out something."

He is a good man.

She leaned back and inhaled the fresh scent of his soap. The fight had left his clothes ripped and his body bruised. He'd changed now and insisted the shower revived him. Even asked her to join him in the stall, but she couldn't.

She leaned her head against his thigh and tried to rub the pain out of her eyes. "I'm fine."

"I'm not convinced."

Neither was she. "Did you come up with the list?"

"We can talk about it another time."

So tempting. "It won't end until we do."

Jonas exhaled hard enough to ruffle her hair. "You're allowed to take a break."

She tipped her head back and looked up at him. "Am I?"

He dropped a quick kiss on her mouth then straightened up again. "It looks like a bunch of leads were called into the hotline back then, but the detectives only looked into six people other than your father very seriously."

"Who were the lucky ones to make the list?"

"You, a neighbor, two unrelated males with violent pasts and long criminal records who were in the area at the time of the murders, Tad Willis and your dad's business partner, Kurt Handler."

Nothing new there. She'd heard all of that before. "The police cleared them all."

"A few of the suspects had some trouble with your dad. He fired Willis and fought with your neighbor."

"And the business with Handler was in financial trouble." She'd found that out years later, but it didn't matter because there wasn't anything for Kurt to gain.

"The other two guys are nasty but seem remote." Jonas sat down next to her on the couch and pulled her legs onto his lap. "What does your gut tell you?"

The intimate position woke up her cells and had her mind sparking back to life. "Still Willis."

"Why?"

"He was at the house that day and lied about it. He'd been fired and lied about it. Lying seemed to be his one skill."

"Not exactly great evidence for homicide."

"He had been accused of attacking another customer. And he did kill himself." She rattled off the evidence she'd memorized long ago.

Now she wondered if Cade carried around a similar mental list that implicated her father. Facts could be twisted and interpreted to fit any argument.

Jonas smoothed his hand up her pants leg and massaged her calf. "Tell me about the partner."

She balanced her head against the back of the couch and let her muscles unwind as Jonas rubbed them. "Dad's best friend. They knew each other in college, worked for other people then branched out together."

"You said there was money trouble."

Her eyes had just closed when they popped open again. "I got the money."

It wasn't a huge amount, but it got her through college and provided the financial safety to go into illustration and live off the early meager payments for her work.

"You got the money because you lived. What if you hadn't?"

She'd run through this scenario a million times and couldn't pin anything on Kurt. It didn't take a genius to know the business partner was as likely as the sole surviving child to be a suspect. But the facts didn't work.

"He was never the beneficiary of Dad's estate. He got the business because of the way the corporation documents were set up, but that turned out to be a financial burden since the business wasn't up and running and was encumbered with debt."

Jonas's eyebrow lifted. "He's a millionaire now."

"Looks like you did your homework on the people in my past."

"It's both my job and the best way to keep you safe."

Jonas's words gave her comfort. Everything from his scent

to his look—heck, even his gun, made her feel safe. "Kurt's financial status is new. It didn't exist then. He got rich in a real-estate boom and has been sitting on a pile of money since."

"Some might say convenient."

"He was a good businessman."

"That could be, but is there any chance I could see the business paperwork? Do you have anything or did Kurt get all of it?"

"I received all of the documents from the police about a month ago thanks to a request I filed, and I discovered some more files mixed in with my parents' things in storage."

"Where is all of that now?"

"Since you insisted we leave my house with more than one file, it's all upstairs in the stacks we brought over."

Jonas groaned. "That's a pretty significant stack. Like, four boxes."

"Don't feel like dragging them downstairs?" She couldn't blame him. The man had been battered and bruised since meeting her. It was a wonder he could even stand up and keep moving by now.

"Just wishing Rich was here so I could order him to do it."

She gave Jonas her most sympathetic look. "Poor baby."

His hand slid higher on her leg. "You can make it up to me later."

"Is that right?"

"I was hoping that was part of the reason you wanted to stay." He leaned in and kissed her.

Those warm lips pressed against hers and she was lost. Hot and demanding, his mouth crossed over hers until her hands gripped his shoulders. His strength radiated off of him and seeped into her.

When they broke apart, her breath hitched in her throat.

"You have a gun and these big shoulders. Any woman with a brain would stick around."

"Thanks." He coughed. "I think."

"But, honestly, I could get that from any of the men you work with." When he scowled, she rushed to fix her babbling. "From you I get something else."

"What is that, other than a guy who carries boxes around?"

"Fire."

A sexy smile spread across his lips. "Interesting. Is that true?"

The man was fishing for compliments and she was inclined to give them. "You have to ask?"

He leaned over and pushed her deep into the couch cushions. "I'll work later."

"No." She gave him a quick kiss then smacked against his shoulders in a gentle shove. "Work now. Fun later. I'll even get up and join you."

"We could shift that to-do list around. Start with the fun then double back. It would clear our heads." He wiggled his eyebrows at her. "Like running."

"Oh, please."

"Exercise is good for you."

She had to ignore the charm and dig down deep for her common sense. "We'd never get to the work. Besides, Rich is coming over."

Jonas blew out a long breath and shot her a woe-is-me frown. "I hate that guy sometimes."

"No, you don't. And you have no one to blame but yourself. You invited him." She pointed in the direction of the kitchen. "Now go make some coffee so we can be at least half-awake for his next research session."

With one last kiss, Jonas took off to do her bidding. She'd just managed to struggle to her feet when her cell phone vibrated against the couch cushion. She saw the number and almost called out to Jonas to let him know Ellie was checking in. Then she read the message.

Jonas in danger. Don't say anything. Come to bookstore alone.

Courtney blinked and reread the three sentences. The words didn't make any sense. He was right there with her.

The dire warnings didn't sound like Ellie. The whole thing felt more like a setup than a real request for help.

The phone shook in her hand.

Hurry.

She stared at the entrance to the kitchen. If she called out, he'd come running. If she needed him to shoot someone or fight to the death, he'd do it.

A sharp pain in her stomach nearly knocked her over. She could put him in danger or she could check this one out alone first. Or she could do a compromise and get a head start, go in and look and have him come right behind her.

She typed out a text but didn't hit Send.

Get to the bookstore now.

Tiptoeing in stocking feet, she got over to the dining-room table and put her phone down on top of the stack of papers he was working on. He'd see it there. He'd wonder and check it.

Then she grabbed his and her shoes and headed for the door.

"ELLIE?" RICH SHOUTED her name as he tried the front door to her shop again.

The bookstore was locked up tight despite the posted working hours and the open sign hanging in the window. He pressed his face close to the glass and looked around. The lights burned and a book lay open near the cash register.

He shifted his position, trying to get a better view of each row of books. Empty aisles. No one was in there. Probably meant she stepped out for a second and forgot to leave a note.

Jonas would be ticked, but there was nothing Rich could do. He couldn't force the woman to sit in her chair and wait for him to come and find her, though the idea did appeal to him on a raw level.

He turned away from the window, thinking to hang out at the diner across the street for a few minutes until Ellie got back. But something pulled his gaze back to the glass.

There at the front of the fourth row nearest the counter was a woman's shoe on the floor. Despite having four sisters, he wasn't much into women's shoes, but this was a high heel and looked kind of sexy. Ellie had a habit of wearing that spiky type at work. Rich knew because he'd spent more than a little time studying her legs.

He tugged on the door handle one more time and heard the internal lock mechanism bang against the wood. It wasn't going to open. If he broke the glass she'd probably kill him. That left trying the back door into her office.

He slipped into the alley that ran between the bookstore and the closed flower shop next door. When he got to the back of the building he saw her station wagon in the parking space.

Without knocking, he tried the back door and felt a surge of relief when it opened without any trouble. He walked into the small hallway and peeked into the bathroom on the right. *Not in there.* That left her office.

The silence fell over him. Ellie usually played music, top-forty hits that caused him to make jokes about her listening taste. Today he only heard the buzz of the lights above his head.

Everything felt wrong and out of place. Danger buzzed around him until he wondered if the Courtney situation had him paranoid and looking around every corner waiting for trouble.

"Ellie?"

He rounded the corner and stopped. The sight in front of him refused to register in his brain. She sat in her desk chair, wide-eyed and tied up with a gag in her mouth.

"What the hell?" Without thinking, his training temporarily forgotten, he stepped inside the small room with its stacks of books and papers piled everywhere.

He realized too late she threw a bug-eyed stare at a space just over his shoulder. His hand hit his gun just as something smashed against his skull.

The blackness swallowed him whole before he could say a thing or call on his radio for help.

Chapter Twenty-Two

Jonas stepped out of the kitchen with two mugs of near-boiling hot coffee in his hands and entered an empty room. He hoped Courtney had decided to lie down, but he guessed she was dragging those boxes out so he could look at the business files she'd asked for.

He groaned. What he really wanted was to take her to bed, but that desire warred with the need to keep her safe. The day had spun out of control so fast that he was desperate to get the investigation back on track.

A pounding crash sounded at his front door. The thumping didn't let up. Rich would ring once and then stand there waiting, and that was only on those occasions where he forgot the key. He had one as a precaution. So this had to be something else.

Jonas put the mugs down on the dining-room table and headed for the door. He took a quick glance out the small window and his amusement faded. Whipping the door open, he stared at Cade.

Gone was the jittery, downtrodden agent. Cade held a gun and wore his protective vest. He was all business.

And, as far as Jonas was concerned, a dead man. He'd given Cade the chance to run and he hadn't taken it. Now he would pay.

"You have to come with me," Cade said, his voice deep and serious.

"You have two seconds to get out of here." Jonas knew he could strangle this man with his bare hands.

The fact Cade ignored the warning at the station sent Jonas's temper soaring. Knowing the man was once again so close to Courtney filled Jonas with a killing rage.

Cade finally focused on Jonas and his eyes widened. "Wait a second."

"You're done here."

Cade held up his free hand. "Listen to me. Courtney is in trouble."

The air stopped moving. "Where is she?"

"That's what I'm trying to tell you."

Jonas grabbed Cade by the collar and dragged him in the house. Slamming him against the back of the door, Jonas stared Cade down. "Give me a reason I shouldn't kill you."

"I'm with the FBI."

"That's not helping your case."

"I can help you find her."

"She's here."

"No."

Cade finally had hit on the one word that would buy him time before Jonas punched him. But the conversation didn't make any sense.

Jonas called for her. When he didn't get an answer on the first try, he yelled again.

"I'm telling you she's not here," Cade said.

Jonas shoved Cade against the door hard enough to make the man's head bounce. "You'll tell me where she is and I'll only break your legs."

"Not me. I didn't do it."

"You say that a lot. You're not the type to take responsibility for anything, are you?"

"Listen to me."

Jonas squeezed his hands closer together, ready to choke off Cade's air if that's what it took to get an honest answer. "I won't be dumb enough to fall for your line a second time."

Cade grabbed for Jonas's hands and tried to pull them off his neck. The gun waved close to Jonas's cheek, and he slapped it away.

"Cade. Now."

"She opened the front door and ran—"

Anger exploded in a fireworks display of red behind Jonas's eyes. "You're still watching the house?"

"I've been watching her for years. It's a hard habit to break."

"I warned you."

"And if someone is really hunting her, and it sounded like there was, I wanted to know who because that could give me the answers I need about my dad."

Jonas leaned in close enough to see the fear skip across Cade's mouth. "Last time, Willis. Where is she?"

"I don't know. I saw her leave and followed. When she ducked around corners, I figured she could be in trouble and came here to get you. I didn't think she'd welcome a rescue from me." Cade got a better grip on Jonas's hands but still couldn't break the hold. "We have to go before we lose her trail."

Jonas pushed Cade against the door one last time then let go. "You think you're coming with me?"

"No matter what else you think, I am trained for this sort of thing. I can help you find her and keep her out of trouble. And I'm telling you that your lady was headed straight into trouble."

Jonas pointed at the dead center of the man's chest. "If she's hurt, if anything has happened to her, I'm going to kill you. I won't wait to gather evidence. You will die."

"You're threatening a federal officer."

"I'm making you a promise." Jonas looked around for his new phone.

He still hadn't found the old one and had grabbed this one from work. Good thing he'd punched in the numbers he needed. He'd call Rich on the way for backup he could trust.

He thought he left it in the kitchen but saw it on the dining-room table and jogged over to get it. He'd taken two steps before he realized it felt wrong in his hand. Bigger. He brought up the screen and touched the display.

Get to the bookstore now.

He glanced up at Cade. "Did she go left or right on the sidewalk?"

"Right."

"She left me a message." Jonas turned the phone around for Cade to see.

The facts didn't make any sense. They were sitting there a second ago, him plotting the fastest way to get her into bed. Now she was on the run. He thought they'd gotten past all that. And then this message and her leaving her phone behind. None of it made sense.

"Check through her call history. She left that message for a reason, and her incoming log might tell you why."

Jonas scrolled through the texts and saw Ellie's warnings. Jonas immediately knew the truth. Someone lured Courtney to the bookstore. And she went. Her recklessness made his knees buckle.

He slipped the phone in his pocket and headed for the door. "Between here and the bookstore, you might want to do some praying."

"Why?"

"Because if we don't find her and fast, I'm blaming the first person I see. That will be you."

COURTNEY WALKED up to the front door of the bookstore and hesitated. She'd spent most of the past few days bugging Jonas about using backup, and here she was walking into what she knew was a trap. Still, her friend was in danger, and Courtney could not handle one more injury suffered on her behalf.

And Jonas would be here soon.

He'd come out of the kitchen, see the message and get over here fast. Hopefully with a platoon of police cars and lots of men with guns.

Oh, how priorities changed when everything fell apart. She'd spent her life blaming the police, and now she was desperate for their assistance.

She pulled the door open and grabbed the bells over the door so they wouldn't chime. Stepping inside, she closed the door without so much as a click.

A steady rock beat thumped. She couldn't hear the lyrics, but she guessed Ellie had the radio on in the back as usual. The one thing missing was Ellie. She didn't sit on her usual stool by the counter. She had the front door open and didn't pop out with a greeting.

Definitely a trap.

With soft steps, Courtney walked through the aisles, looking around each corner and scanning the back wall as she went. The temptation to call out for Ellie swamped her, but Courtney beat it back. Announcing her presence could spell trouble for both of them.

The fact Ellie wasn't waiting at the door told Courtney what she needed to know. Confirmed her fears and sent her heart speeding into danger territory.

She stopped when the tile floor creaked. The sound didn't come from her. She whipped around, looking for any sign that she wasn't alone. Only high shelves greeted her. The books Ellie loved so much closed in on her, as if moving in the space without any help from anyone, and blocked Courtney's view of the front door.

When she turned back around, she heard the crackle of a radio. She recognized the sound, a police radio. It went off every few seconds in Jonas's house. He turned it down while they ate, but the information came in fast and steady on police frequencies. Calls from Aberdeen, from Bartholomew County and from the surrounding areas.

But that didn't make sense. The noise didn't fit the setting.

She reached the cash register and saw Ellie's book open on the desk. Glancing into the doorway beyond, Courtney saw only an empty office. Fighting back the fear streaming through her blood, she stepped inside. Her foot hit against something. Someone. A hand from where Rich sprawled on the floor.

"No." She dropped to her knees and searched for a pulse. A steady beat pounded under her fingers.

A shuffling in the hall grabbed her attention. Leaning forward, she spotted a woman's bare foot and men's black dress shoes. Someone stood just out of sight and held Ellie.

Courtney opened her mouth as her fingers pressed against Rich's side searching for a weapon.

"Courtney!"

Jonas's shout had her jumping off the floor, cracking her knee against the tile. A woman's scream—Ellie—and the bang of the back door followed. Courtney didn't know where to look. When she spun around to the back again, Ellie lay slumped against the hallway wall and the man's shoes were gone.

Courtney's head spun. "Jonas, back here."

Footsteps thudded. He burst into the room with his gun raised. Then he glanced down, took in the bodies and swore. He dropped down beside her and ran his hands over Rich.

"What are you doing?"

"Checking for broken bones." Anger vibrated off of Jonas as he spoke.

"I think he got hit in the head." She held out her palms and showed Jonas the blood. "It's his."

Jonas glanced over to his left. "What about her?"

She scrambled on her hands and knees to her friend. Ellie's chest lifted and fell, and Courtney almost collapsed in relief. She looked Ellie over for blood and didn't see anything. "I think the guy knocked her out before he ran."

"What?" Jonas's laserlike stare came back to Courtney. All that intensity focused solely on her. "He was still here when you came in?"

Seeing the fury darken his eyes, she almost hated to tell him the truth. She knew what came next. The big chase. The part where he got hurt.

But the only way to end this was with more death or a capture. She prayed for the latter. "He just took off out the back door."

Jonas frowned at her as he stood up. "Who?"

"I didn't see him."

Rich moaned and Jonas nodded in his direction. "Take care of him. We'll discuss your decision to come here without me later."

"I knew you'd—"

His jaw clenched. "Not now. I can't do it now and concentrate."

Now she knew. He was furious at the situation…and with her. She'd worry about that later. Now she needed Jonas here with her and not chasing down a killer on his own. "We need an ambulance."

"Hold right here." Jonas slipped out of the room.

Courtney didn't wait. She reached up to Ellie's desk and

fumbled for the phone. Her hand hit it and she tugged, bringing it crashing down to the floor.

She called the emergency number and gave the information. She heard sirens seconds later.

With the initial chaos over, she slumped back against the wall and cradled Rich's head on her lap. From the look of the two victims she knew he was worse off. The blood finally turned to a trickle after she pressed the end of her shirt to it.

The attacker could circle around and come back, but she doubted it. She had all the time in the world to panic about Jonas as she waited. Her heart slowed until she thought she'd pass out. The idea of him being hurt, of her being without him, made her gag.

In just a few days, she'd fallen for him. She'd picked the guy who rushed in when everyone else rushed out. The one type of guy she'd vowed never to love.

She thought about a world without him in it, and everything inside her went dark and cold.

At the sound of footsteps, her heart leaped and her fingers tingled. She turned her head ready with a smile and saw Cade step into the back hallway. Relief gave way to panic. The trembling started low in her belly and spread from there.

Then another emotion took over.

Rage filled her until a swath of red zoomed in front of her eyes. "You!"

"What happened in here?" He looked around, oblivious to her anger, and crouched in front of Ellie.

"Do not touch her."

His shocked gaze flew to Courtney's face at her scream. He held out his hands in that calming gesture all law-enforcement professionals seemed to use. The same one that drove her nuts.

"I'm here to help," he said.

Liar. This time she knew. The moment of her dropping

her guard and believing had passed. "You could have killed them with those blows."

Jonas walked in while issuing orders into his radio. He lowered it to do a visual tour of the room. "I missed him."

She pointed at Cade. "He is right in front of you! Arrest him!"

Cade and Jonas stared at each other, then at her.

Jonas stepped over Cade and walked over to her. Balancing on the balls of his feet, he met her at eye level. "I can't do that."

The room started to spin again. The air shifted and whatever was inside her head moved a second behind when she turned. "Why not?"

"Cade didn't do it."

She'd created this mess. She's convinced Jonas that Cade deserved a second chance. Now he was scamming them all. "You think he just happened to be here? Notice how people get hurt and he's always looming nearby. That's not a coincidence. My initial worries about him were right. Take him in before he hurts someone else."

Jonas put a hand over hers. "I know he's not the attacker because he came with me."

"What?"

"He's the reason I got to you in time."

Chapter Twenty-Three

The police crawled all over the bookstore. The emergency care workers checked on Ellie and had Rich strapped to a stretcher, over his profanity-filled objections. The deafening rumble of chatter and clicking of first-responder radios blocked out the music on Ellie's radio.

Jonas took a few minutes to watch it all unfold. Doing anything else would invite a whole lot of yelling. By him.

He stood with his arm resting on the cash register and struggled to cool his temper before he talked with Courtney in private. She hovered over Ellie, getting in the way of the ambulance crew and apologizing to her friend with every other word.

Courtney's position put her on the exact opposite side of the store from Cade. He hung around, watching and waiting, taking it all in without saying a word.

Jonas knew he owed Cade on this one. Threatening to kill him probably ranked as one of those things Jonas needed to apologize for. And he would, but later. Right now his attention was on Courtney and the way she studiously avoided him.

She hadn't rushed over or looked at him since the initial skirmish when the police piled through the doors ready to shoot. Her usual ignore-the-instructions personality dimmed.

She was in scurry-around mode. She likely feared if she stopped moving he would catch her. And he would.

As she bounced around, his gaze wandered over her. She had her hair piled high on her head in a ponytail. Blood caked on the bottom of her T-shirt. Rich's blood.

The bright stain set off a new round of pounding in Jonas's head. He stalked over to her, counting to ten and then starting over in the hope of wrestling his anger under control. He tried to keep his mind open and his jaw unlocked.

By the time he touched her arm, a lecture hours long filled his brain. "Enough avoiding the topic. Care to tell me?"

That was all he said. She didn't pretend to misunderstand, which likely saved them from a full-on fight. "I had to go when I saw the text."

Not good enough. "I was right there. You could have told me and let me handle it. We could have called in Rich and possibly prevented him being hurt in the first place." Jonas knew that last part wasn't fair, and the way she winced, he knew he hit his target, but he needed her to understand the gravity of the situation.

A killer roamed the area and she ran around as if no one could touch her. Even though it all related back to her.

"I didn't want you hurt," she said, pleading as she spoke.

"Excuse me?"

She rested a hand against his stomach, right at the top of his belt. "You're not the only one who can protect, you know."

The touching threw him off for a second. Being this close, smelling the shampoo in her hair, made his brain stutter. He stepped back to keep from wrapping her in his arms. This was the wrong place and definitely the wrong time for that.

Enough with the fighting and with all those other emotions that battered him whenever he saw her. It was time to make a drastic move. "I have to get you out of here."

"The bookstore?"

"Out of Aberdeen and all of the danger surrounding you."

"Absolutely not!" she shouted. Several people glanced in their direction.

He dragged her with him behind the counter. With all the people buzzing around, privacy wasn't possible. Crowding in tight qualified as the closest he could get to her.

And he had to make her understand. He'd use any tool at his disposal at this point—guilt, anger or whatever else it took. If he had to tie her up and rush her to safety, he would. He'd rather apologize later than see her in danger now.

"This person who is after you, whoever it is, is using and attacking people you care about. There are no boundaries for this guy. Everyone is a potential victim." He stared at her, willing her to understand. "And we can't blame Cade for this round. It's someone else, which is even scarier because I don't have a lead."

"How did he end up with you?"

"Instead of questioning him, you should thank him. He's the one who told me you were missing." After a lifetime of hating each other, Cade may have saved her. The sharp change in the course of their lives wasn't lost on Jonas.

"No, that's not right."

He refused to spend another minute arguing about this and hoped to shut it down with a firm response. "Yes."

She grabbed onto his forearms. "You were supposed to read the text and come get me. How did Cade get involved?"

"He knocked on the door. And it's a good thing he did because if I waited to find the phone it might have been too late. Remember that for next time you want to sneak off."

Her shoulders fell. "I'm kind of hoping there won't be a next time."

"Me, too, but I know better."

She nibbled on her bottom lip as she looked around the

room. The place resembled military triage. Jonas counted heads and calculated that every officer in Aberdeen was in the room. More than a few of Walt's sheriffs also wandered around.

Jonas hoped there wouldn't be any crime in the county today.

"Where would I go?" She asked the question in a put-upon voice.

"With Walt."

Her gaze shot to where the older man stood at the bookstore's front door then back to Jonas again. "How am I safer with him? The guy hates me."

"He's the sheriff."

"And?"

Jonas wasn't in the mood to take on her police phobia, so he let the comment drop. "You'll be out of Aberdeen and only Rich, Walt and I will know where you are."

Jonas wanted to kick himself for not making this move sooner. Walt had offered, but he'd couched the suggestion in comments about Jonas's private life and Jonas had gotten defensive. Everything got tangled up and confused. He'd let his ego get in the way and pushed off Walt's concerns. Now Jonas knew that had been a mistake.

"And where will you be?" she asked.

"Getting information from Ellie and trying to track this attacker down. The town isn't that big. Someone must have seen him. I just need a decent description. Once I have a sketch, I'll send it to Walt for you to review." That all required Jonas to not have Courtney by his side.

Whether he liked the outcome or not—and he didn't—he needed his full concentration on this. Worrying about her sucked up most of his energy. While he'd be edgy with her at Walt's place, at least Jonas could put every minute of every hour into ending this thing.

Then she could come back and they'd figure out the what-happens-next part. But he couldn't get there until he walked through this.

"It's the best way." The words, ragged and raw, tore out of him.

If she chewed any harder on that lip, she'd draw blood. "Who is going to keep Ellie safe?"

"Rich volunteered." Jonas found his first smile. "A little fast, I might add."

Courtney looked around Jonas. He followed her gaze and saw Rich throw off the tube plugged into his arm and go to Ellie. When he sat next to her, she leaned in with her head on his shoulder.

Courtney's mouth dropped open. "Those two? She never said anything."

Jonas nodded. "Surprised me, too. I knew he found her attractive but didn't know he'd made a move."

Courtney put a hand on his jaw and brought his gaze back to her. "I don't want to leave you."

"I'm not going anywhere." Jonas held her hand against his skin, letting her soft touch soothe him. "This is temporary. We catch this guy, drag him out of town, and then I think you mentioned something about naked wrestling."

She chuckled. "I most certainly didn't."

"Huh, really? Well, think about it while you're gone."

"I'm going to try not to."

"I expect you to miss me." The words slipped out before he could stop them. They hung there, open and ready to crush him.

But the light in her face never dimmed. "Only if that will be a very mutual missing."

He didn't have to think about his answer. "It will."

"Then we have a deal."

"Good." *Great, fantastic.* The words tripped on hi tongue, but he shoved them back when Walt stepped up.

He clapped a hand against Jonas's back as he stared a Courtney. "Are you ready to head out?"

"I know you don't like me, but—"

Walt held up a hand. "I don't have a problem with you."

Jonas didn't believe it but he appreciated the attempt t calm her nerves. "Thanks."

Walt nodded. "Whatever it takes to end this, we're going to do it."

COURTNEY STEPPED into Walt's family room and frowned She'd expected a rush of relief at being somewhere safe an away, but nothing came.

The place was nice enough, a low-slung ranch house out side of Aberdeen. Acres of open land surrounded the place A forgotten swing hung from the tree just out front.

On the inside, heavy furniture, very dark and at least tw decades old, filled the room. There were cabinets filled wit tiny figurines and stuffed animals over the mantel. It wa all very feminine. Collections gathered over time and store with the utmost care.

Not exactly the decor she expected from a lifetim lawman.

She walked down the two steps into the sunken living room and went to the fireplace. The blue bear on the en wore a shirt stamped with the hospital logo. She traced he fingers over the letters then picked up the bear, letting he fingers squeeze into the fluffy softness.

"My wife was sick for a long time."

Courtney jumped at Walt's voice. He stood right behin her.

Jonas had filled her in on the general details, but seeing

he loss in Walt's sad eyes brought it all home. "I'm really orry about your wife."

"The disease ravaged her then lingered. She spent two ears going in and out of the hospital, unable to walk and ventually unable to do anything for herself."

Pain filled every word. Courtney recognized the slight remor. Sometimes, lost in her own darkness, she forgot that thers lived in a similar hell. Her heart twisted for him.

This man served as a father figure to Jonas. Walt meant omething to the man she'd started to love, so he meant omething to her, too.

"That must have been terrible." Courtney rubbed a hand ver Walt's arm.

"A slow death is devastating in so many ways."

She only knew about a calculated assault. The wounds eft from that never healed. "I can imagine."

"Emotionally and financially it ruins you."

She didn't know what to say, so she didn't say anything. Walt's entire body slumped as he dropped into a big eather chair in front of her. "It wasn't supposed to go like his."

"What?"

"You." Walt took out his gun and balanced it on his lap. "Me?"

"He was supposed to do a wellness check and leave." 'ain turned to anger with each word Walt uttered. "I never hought he'd get messed up in your life."

The blood left her head. "What are you saying?"

"Jonas wasn't supposed to be involved. I didn't want him urt, but I needed him to go in that first time."

She tightened her hold on the stuffed bear. "You're in-olved in all of this?"

"I was paid to deliver you. That was all this was ever supposed to be. Me getting you to the guy who wanted you. Walt motioned for her to sit down across from him. "And am going to do that now."

Chapter Twenty-Four

Jonas forced his legs to move. Seeing Courtney walk away, glance over her shoulder and smile nearly dropped him to his knees. Emotions battled inside him and none of them were relief. That sensation didn't come as he expected.

But he could only handle one issue right now, and this one would be tough to choke out. Admitting he was wrong was not one of Jonas's skills.

He stepped up to Cade. "Now might be a good time to thank you."

Cade stopped staring at the floor and looked up. The haze over his eyes hadn't cleared, but this wasn't confusion. Jonas knew the look. The other man was in deep-thinking mode. Jonas doubted Cade had even heard the apology.

"What is it? What's in your head?" Jonas asked.

"Who came into the room after me?"

Jonas had no idea where Cade mentally wandered in the timeline. "What?"

"You said you saw me go in and out of Paul's hospital room. Okay, that's not a secret. I went in to talk with him. But who else walked in there?"

Jonas didn't have an answer, but he wanted to see where the question went. "What are you thinking?"

"What's going on?" Rich joined them.

Jonas took in the limp and the way his friend held his head

and recognized the signs of a guy refusing to stay down. "Should you be up?"

Rich shrugged. "I am."

Cade faced them both with his hands out, as if trying to convince them of something. "The guard was there and alive when I left Paul's room. That leaves a small window for someone else to sneak in there."

Jonas understood the obsession. Cade had lost a friend and wanted answers. He'd jumped into the investigation and had the determined look of a man who had no intention of getting out again until the mystery had been solved.

A kick of admiration hit Jonas. If Cade was in, so was the Aberdeen police force.

"It would have to be someone with access." Cade nodded, clearly picking up speed on his theory. "Someone who could get by without any questions and who knew exactly when to get to the door because Stimpson would be gone, or knew Stimpson well enough to get in with permission."

"That sounds like an inside job," Rich said.

Cade snapped his fingers. "Who has the tape?"

"There are two. The official one and mine, and the county sheriff has them both."

Cade's eyes narrowed. "The guy who called me about Paul?"

"We only saw the tape up to the point where you came out of the room," Rich explained.

The fact tickled in the back of Jonas's brain. He'd been so quick to jump on Cade as a suspect, he never thought to ask more questions or insist on seeing every moment of that room for hours on each end. He saw Cade come out and then the empty doorway.

If the guard was there when Cade came out, why didn't the tape show it? "The guard was still there," he repeated.

Cade coughed. "I already said that. Several times, in fact."

The pieces clicked together in Jonas's mind. The timing fell into place. "If Stimpson had been outside of the room when Paul was killed he would have heard something."

Rich leaned against the wall, likely to keep from falling down again. "Maybe Stimpson did it."

Jonas shook his head. "Then why is he dead? No, it's more likely Stimpson was a pawn. The guy was paid or was asked to look the other way."

Jonas knew that had to be it. Stimpson's role was minor at best. He could finger someone, tie a person to that room, and he died for it, but he didn't do the killing.

"We need to see that tape," Cade said.

Rich reached for his radio but he grabbed air because it wasn't on his shoulder. "I'll call Walt."

Jonas grabbed his friend's arm when he signaled to another officer. "Skip Walt. Use the landline and call hospital security. Tell the head of security to upload the duplicate copy and send it to your cell."

"I have your video on my phone already."

"Good. That one might give us a different angle. We'll check out both." Jonas looked at Rich and Cade. "I want this immediate and quiet."

Rich frowned. "What's with all the secrecy?"

"I don't want anyone else touching the videos but us. The hospital one goes straight from security to us."

"You're including me?" Cade sounded stunned by the thought of being included.

Even ten minutes ago Jonas would have shut him out, but the guy proved to be an asset, and Jonas wasn't one to throw up territorial barriers. He'd take all the help he could get, so long as he knew the motives behind it.

"You're FBI, right?"

Rich continued to shake his head. Understanding washed

over his face. "You think someone tampered with the hospital tape."

Jonas didn't want to think it because the arrow could point anywhere. Any person under his command could be dirty. Missing that, not being able to ferret out that disloyalty before it blew up played on every insecurity he possessed. The failure would once again be his alone.

"All I know is the tape went to the shot of the empty doorway, no Stimpson, after we saw Cade go in and out. I'm thinking that was planted there because it doesn't match the unofficial version." Jonas hitched his chin toward Ellie. "How's she coming with her description?"

The question sidetracked Rich. "I'll check."

Cade waited until they were alone to talk again. "This could get ugly."

Jonas nodded. "It already is."

COURTNEY SAT ACROSS FROM WALT and watched him shift the gun from one hand to the other. "Tell me why."

"I didn't have a choice. The bills destroyed me."

Her throat burned with the need to scream. All that potential wasted over dollars. "This was about money? Stimpson and Eckert are dead because of your need to pay a bill. You do realize that, right?"

Walt shook his head. "I didn't have anything to do with those deaths."

The man compartmentalized and ignored. She hated people who refused to take responsibility for their actions. Right now, she despised Walt for both what he was doing and how he had betrayed Jonas.

"You put me in danger. Worse, you risked Jonas's life by bringing him into this. And all because of money?"

Walt pointed the gun at her. "I told you Jonas wasn't supposed to be involved. He was supposed to knock on the door and plant the woman's name. That's it."

She watched Walt put the facts into neat little boxes. It didn't matter if they fit or not, if they were true or not; he grabbed onto his rationale to get through.

She wanted to rip the safety shield away. "You dropped Jonas right in the middle of it. *You* did that."

But Walt was lost. He talked more to himself than to her. "He'd always been so practical. He follows my advice, except when it comes to you."

Bile filled her mouth. "He's a better police officer than you."

"Oh, please." Walt's stern voice sounded more like a lecturing parent now. "He destroyed his career in Los Angeles. I'm the one who put him back together again."

"What are you talking about?"

"He killed that drug-addicted kid. The press blamed Jonas, then he blew it all in a later case by hesitating when his partner needed him to shoot."

Her heart ripped in two. Actually pulled apart and yanked until the rough edges jabbed at her. Jonas lived with so much and never said a word. "I thought you cared about him. That you viewed him as a son."

Walt swallowed hard enough to make his throat move. "Our relationship isn't your business."

He wasn't just in denial. He was delusional. "You think he's going to like hearing about all you've done?"

"He won't know. You'll be gone and everything will get back to normal." The explanation sounded so rational. Walt acted as if he were reading a train schedule instead of planning the end of her life.

Panic gave way to numbness. She tried to blink the flatness away, but it wouldn't go. She didn't tremble. She felt nothing. "Can you live with all that you've done?"

"I have to."

"What would your wife say?"

His face flushed a deep red. "Don't you dare talk about her."

Going for his love for Jonas hadn't worked, so she tried to appeal to his ego instead. "He says you're one of the best cops he's ever known. He trusts you."

"That's enough." The deep voice rumbled through the room as a hand landed on her shoulder.

She jumped out of the chair. When she glanced to her left the image didn't make sense. Him, here?

"Kurt? What are—"

He walked toward her, pushing her back until the bottom of the brick fireplace hit against her ankles. The gun hovered just out of reach.

"You were supposed to stop digging," Kurt said. "Everything was fine until you got those boxes of business documents."

All the arguments she used with Jonas rushed back into her head. Kurt's name had always been on the list, but everyone discounted him.

He wept at her father's casket and cried with her as she threw the flowers and they lowered the bodies into the ground.

Nothing added up. "I don't understand. You didn't benefit from their deaths."

"I was supposed to. The insurance policy should have named me. I was supposed to be the alternate beneficiary on the estate. That was our deal. Your father promised, even produced fake papers to confirm it, but he lied."

Her father chose his family instead. If she survived this, she'd hold on to that fact for comfort. "And I was supposed to die."

"I should have known you'd sneak out that night." Kurt

shook his head on a laugh. "You were always the troubled one."

She'd been difficult and artsy. She'd bucked her father's discipline and pushed boundaries. But she didn't deserve to die and neither did they.

"You killed my family for money." Saying the words made her chest ache.

"Your father threatened to call the prosecutor. I was going to lose everything."

She'd studied everything and never found even a line about a prosecutor. "What are you talking about?"

"None of that matters now." Walt stood up. "Cade will be here soon and we can end this."

The horrible news just kept coming. Everyone she believed in turned out to want to hurt her. Everyone except Jonas.

"What does Cade have to do with this?" she asked.

Kurt took out a phone and dialed. "He's going to finish the job his father started."

She spun around and faced Walt. Using all her energy she tried to will him to listen to her. "This is the man you're working with?"

"Shut up," Kurt said without lifting his head. "Cade's been waiting to see you."

He doesn't know. The realization shot through her that Kurt missed the part where she had already talked with Cade. Where he had already saved her by getting Jonas to the bookstore in time.

She glanced at Walt, who moved his head in an almost imperceptible shake. She turned back to Kurt and had to ignore his smirk to keep from tackling him and risking a bullet. "You think Cade will come here to kill me?"

"He hates you. When I gave him your address here in

Oregon, he was so grateful. He came right away and has been following you ever since."

Not anymore. He was working with Jonas now.

A call to Cade would tip off Jonas and bring the police crashing in. Walt had to know that, but he wasn't talking. She didn't know what that meant, but she wasn't about to trust him yet.

Kurt shot her a feral smile. "If Cade doesn't kill you, I'll do it for him."

Chapter Twenty-Five

Rich slapped a piece of paper on the counter. "According to Ellie, this is the guy."

Cade studied it. His facial expression never changed. "Kurt Handler."

Jonas had seen one photo of the guy in the case file. He'd been younger, thinner. "The business partner?"

Cade rubbed his neck. "The same guy who told me where I could find Courtney in Oregon."

"What?" The word exploded from Rich's mouth.

Jonas did a slow burn. "You didn't think to tell us that?"

"It seemed to come from a good place. He talked about his love for Courtney and talked about how I needed closure and so did she." Cade looked up at the ceiling and blew out a long breath. "I didn't care about closing anything. I took the information and pretended I'd make up with her...but I guess Kurt was pretending, too."

Jonas could see the regret on the other man's face. Hear it in his voice. "You wanted to get to her and make her stop."

"I thought Kurt was being naive, but I didn't care because his good intentions matched with my schemes. Now I know he was planning something worse than I could imagine."

Rich threw his hands up. "Why?"

Jonas knew enough to answer that one. "He was the busi-

ness partner, so I'm guessing it will all go back to money."
His back teeth slammed together as he said the words.

"I'll put out an APB and see if his office can tell me where
he is," Rich said.

They had to find him another way. The man was close,
so close Jonas felt as if he could smell him. "They'll say he's
somewhere else. The guy came here to cover his tracks on a
mass murder. No one knows he's here. The evidence likely
points to him being somewhere else."

Rich nodded. "So where do we find him?"

"On my cell." Cade stared at his phone as if he didn't
know how it landed in his hand. "It's an address."

That nerve in Jonas's cheek that warned him about danger
started ticking. "Why would Kurt lead us to him?"

"He's leading *me*. He doesn't know I'm with you." Cade
smiled.

Satisfaction soared through Jonas. "And why would you
be? He'd never count on a decade-long feud being in a cease-
fire."

"Let's see where he is so we can plan a strategy." Rich
took the phone. His mouth flattened as he glanced up at
Jonas. "Can't be."

"What?" Jonas asked.

Rich turned the display around so Jonas could read it. "It's
Walt's house."

"Isn't that the guy who gave you the hospital video?" Cade
clicked his tongue against the roof of his mouth. "Interesting."

Jonas wanted to strangle Cade and choke off that sound.
"There's no way."

Rich cleared his throat. "Jonas—"

Icy fear spread through every inch of Jonas's body. His

chest tightened until it was hard to breathe. "He has Court-ney." Anxiety poured through him as he looked at Rich for help. "I gave her to him."

Cade took over. "Then we need to get her out."

"You have a plan?" Jonas asked.

"Always. I go through the back—"

Jonas's brain rebooted. "No, you'll go right through the front door."

THE KNOCK CAME twenty minutes later.

Kurt smiled as he motioned for Walt to get the door. "Showtime."

Courtney prayed she wasn't wrong, that the look she saw on Cade's face in that parking lot and again at the bookstore had been a dawning realization that they both wanted the same thing. If he still carried the same anger he brought with him to town, she was a dead woman.

Kurt would kill Cade, too, but she didn't stand a chance. She now knew too much. Her heart ached at the thought of not seeing Jonas again, but some peace came in knowing he wouldn't be in the middle of this when it happened. He was safe back in Aberdeen.

And Walt remained a wild card. She stared at his back, waiting for him to turn around and shoot Kurt, but it didn't happen. He opened the door.

Cade walked in.

Alone.

The last flicker of hope inside her blew out. He didn't have Jonas behind him or backup ready to go. He'd actually answered Kurt's call to come and get her.

"Cade." Kurt nodded for the younger man to take the seat next to her. "I promised you I'd lead you to her."

"I didn't expect you to be here." Cade's face didn't give anything away.

She didn't see his gun but she expected he had one on him. If he was like Jonas, he had more than one weapon within reaching distance. She just didn't understand why Kurt didn't disarm Cade.

"I told you I wanted closure." Kurt nodded. "This does it."

This was what she was now? "For you," she spit out.

"You never learn." Hate roared out of Kurt when he talked. "Your mouth continues to get you in trouble."

She wondered why she never saw it before. Kurt looked at her and his eyes filled with venom. She spoke and he snarled. Either he'd controlled his reactions until now or she hadn't noticed because she hadn't wanted to see it. She'd been too focused on Tad Willis.

Cade sat up straight with his hands steepled in front of him. "What's the plan here?"

"There's only one way for her to stop pinning the blame on your father." Kurt made a tsk-tsking sound. "You know, she demanded more information and the police gave it to her. It's only a matter of time before she concocts a new story and your father's memory is further diminished."

The tension exploded in her gut. She blurted out the first thing to pop into her head. "He's going to kill you."

Immediately, Kurt turned his gun back on her again. "I told you once to shut up. Don't make me tell you again."

Cade didn't even blink as he looked at Walt. "What's your role here?"

Kurt answered for the older man. "I needed some local talent to make security tapes disappear and plant the seeds so Courtney knew she was about to be found out."

"Why give her the heads-up?" Cade asked.

"The point was to flush her out and make her slip up."

She snorted. "When did that happen?"

"My first guy messed up. I admit that," Kurt said. "Who knew a small-town deputy would step in and cause so much trouble?"

Cade nodded. "Jonas Porter."

Kurt threw his head back and laughed. "I may kill him just for fun."

Walt let out a battle cry and he launched his body at Kurt. Walt got halfway across the room before his body jerked back. He grabbed for his chest as blood spurted through his fingers.

The gun in his hand fell to the carpet with a soft thud. A small O formed on his lips as he dropped to his knees.

"Walt!" She tried to stand up but Cade pulled her back down.

Glass shattered all around her. The windows blew in as a rush of cold air filled the room.

Her brain struggled to make sense of what happened as Cade pushed her to the floor and folded his body over hers. He'd tucked her half under him and half under the coffee table. The weight shoved her into the carpet while his gun dug into her leg.

She heard shouts and gunfire. She looked up in time to see Jonas run through the door to the kitchen and hit Kurt in the side. The men went flying, smashing into the brick fireplace before they rolled to the floor.

Jonas got off one punch, then a second. Blood rushed from Kurt's nose and he screamed for help. Jonas kept hitting until Rich grabbed him from behind.

She could hear heavy breathing and crashing sounds as glass and drywall fell to the floor. Cade swore in her ear but didn't move, no matter how hard she shoved and how loudly she yelled for him to let go.

Rich's voice broke into the chaos, ordering people to move

here and there and calling for a medic. Shouts of "Officer down" filled the room. Sirens wailed around them, and uniformed officers poured in from every direction.

One second she moved her head to keep her jaw from squishing into the carpet, the next the weight lifted off her back. A hand picked her off the floor and arms gathered her against a strong chest.

Jonas. She recognized his scent and the hard planes of his body.

"You came." She whispered the words over and over against his chest.

"I'll always be here." He kissed her forehead then her eyelids.

"Walt?"

She felt a tremor run under her hands. "The crew is working on him."

She buried her head in his neck. "I'm so sorry."

"Not your fault." A breath shuddered in his chest. "My fault."

"This is not over." Kurt issued his threat as Rich wrestled him into cuffs and forced him to stand up.

Cade walked right up to the other man. "Yeah, it is. I wanted the person who ruined my father, and now I have him. You."

"Do you know who I am?" Disdain dripped from Kurt's mouth and hung on his words.

Courtney couldn't look at him. The hatred she felt threatened to spill over and ruin everything.

"I will ruin you, Jonas Porter."

Before she could say anything, Jonas moved. He grabbed Kurt around the neck. "You are nothing more than a killer and I will tell everyone—prosecutor, reporter, *your kids*—

whoever will listen. You destroyed a family for greed and now you will lose everything. I will make sure of it."

Kurt tried to weasel out of the hold. "You can't do this."

Jonas nodded to Rich. "Get him out of here."

Chapter Twenty-Six

Jonas paced the floor of the hospital. Walt had been in surgery for hours. The doctors talked about internal injuries and loss of blood. A few minutes before, a nurse had come out and said everything was fine and that the surgeon would be out soon.

Courtney still couldn't process it all. So much destruction and uncertainty, all over money. The strain of being furious and sad at the same time sapped all of her reserves.

But when Jonas sat down next to her and grabbed for her hand, the world righted again. Staring at their linked fingers on his lap, she wondered what was going on in his head.

For her, the questions had been answered. She had the pieces from her past. Healing would come later. Now her life focused on her future. And she wanted Jonas in it.

She leaned her head on his shoulder. "I think I could sleep for a week."

"Longer."

The idea of running off with him and enjoying the sunshine and the water brought a smile to her face. "Any chance you have vacation time coming?"

He flinched at her words.

She lifted her head. "What is it?"

"I almost got you killed."

Here it was, the guilt she knew was pinging around inside

him. Until they moved past this, until he dealt with his past and agreed to put it behind him, they were stuck treading water.

"No, you saved me. Kurt tried to kill me. And more than once, which is something I still can't believe." The words tasted foul in her mouth.

She'd grieved with him and his family, spent holidays at his house. The whole time he hated her and wanted her dead. She had no idea how to deal with that information. She could write him off as crazy, but he wasn't. The answers were just not that simple.

"Cade made sure you didn't get injured while you were in that room." Jonas had filled her in on the whole plan but repeated it now.

Cade went in so the other men could get set. When he said Jonas's full name, that was the signal to start moving. Falling on her was Cade's way of protecting her when everything went nuts.

"I didn't know what side he was on when he walked into that room. But I knew Walt's pretending not to know that you and Cade were working together was a good sign."

"I'm not sure what to say about the Walt piece." Jonas rubbed his chest with his free hand. "But Cade insisted on being there and protecting you. I think it was his penance."

"He didn't have to do it, but I sure appreciate it. Before he leaves town I have to figure out a way to apologize for what I did to his father."

"His father made his own choice. That wasn't your fault."

"Think Cade will see it that way?"

"I think he will now." Jonas lifted their hands to his mouth and kissed her wrist. "We all owe you."

"For what?"

"I made you go with Walt—"

It was all too much. She pulled her hand away and stood up. "Stop."

"What?"

"I'm not doing this."

Jonas frowned, which was all that he'd done since he watched the workers load Walt into the ambulance. "I don't know what you're talking about."

She'd lived so many days in the dark. Now she wanted to walk in the light. She wanted to be healthy and have a future. She wanted all of that with Jonas, but he had to meet her partway.

"I know it's ridiculous and I don't understand it myself, but I love you." There, she'd said it. The words came out and she had no regrets either for what she felt or for saying them.

"Courtney—"

"But I'm done living with what could have been. It's time to restore what I can and move on from the rest. I need to forgive myself for being the survivor." She choked back a sob that rushed up on her and threatened to overtake her voice. "And you need to let yourself off the hook for all the horrors of the world."

She waved him off when he reached for her. If he touched her, her resolve would crumble. She had to say it all first. "You didn't kill Henry. You didn't make Walt turn or take Kurt's money offer. You didn't hurt me."

Jonas's head dropped. "It's not that simple."

"Yeah, it actually is." She picked her purse off the floor.

"Where are you going?"

"Home. Come and get me when you're ready to move on." She took the hardest steps of her life. The ones that took her away from him.

Two hours later Jonas slammed his car door and headed for his front steps. He'd been all over the county. He waited at

Courtney's house. Actually broke her back window to get in when no one answered. He'd called Ellie and even checked in with Cade to see if he knew—

"About time you got here. I was beginning to think you were going to be thick about this." Courtney's voice floated down to him from above.

Jonas looked up, convinced he was dreaming.

She was on his porch. Sitting on the big lawn chair shivering as the wind whipped across the porch.

She pointed at the door. "I'm going to need a key."

"Done." He'd give her the deed to the place if she wanted it.

She smiled and laid her head against the back of the chair. "That was easy."

"What are you doing here?"

"Ellie said you were looking for me."

"Where were you?"

"Here the whole time." Courtney exhaled, giving him her best you-are-so-clueless look. "Technically I know this is your home, but I think of it as mine now."

The words erased the anxiety that had been humming through him since she walked out. "I can live with that."

"It's comfortable. You're comfortable."

"Never thought I'd be so happy to have a woman call me that." He jogged up the steps.

Crossing the threshold to the porch was like breaking through a barrier. Once he got close to her, he saw the shy mix of a smile and wariness on her face. She actually thought he might push her away.

Not going to happen.

"How's Walt?" she asked.

Jonas wasn't ready to talk about that topic. Not yet. But he knew with her help the pain would ease. Everything else pulsed and grew brighter around her. It was only right that the hurt would dim.

"He'll pull through. Rich is getting his statement. Cade is answering questions from his superiors, but I don't care about any of that."

"What do you care about?"

He lifted her out of the chair and sat back down with her curled on his lap. "You."

She wrapped her arms around his neck. "Good answer."

"I want what you want."

Her fingers slipped into his hair. "What is that?"

He put a hand on her legs to keep her from squirming. Much more of that and he wouldn't say what he needed to say. "A real life."

"With me."

"Yeah, since I love you, it makes sense it would be with you."

Her mouth dropped open and her eyes filled with tears. "Love?"

"I'm pretty sure I started falling when you ran from me and climbed over that fence."

"That was pretty sexy, huh?"

"The combination of strong and smart and beautiful felled me." From the beginning he didn't have any shield against her. She rushed through life and around his rules, and he found her irresistible.

"What happens now?"

He brushed his lips over her mouth and marveled at how quickly the heat built between them. "First, we go upstairs and spend a little time in our bed."

"It's a good mattress."

He put his hand over hers to stop her from unbuttoning his shirt to his waist. Though it was tempting to sit out there naked, the good people of Aberdeen needed a better example from the deputy police chief. There would be enough problems with whispering thanks to Walt's poor decisions.

"After the bed, which I'm thinking will take four or five days, we'll talk about the big things." He nibbled on her neck.

Her head tilted to the side to give him more room. "Like?"

"Living arrangements, our future, marriage and possibly expanding the family."

She stared at him, her big eyes wet. "Family."

He put her hand over his heart and made the most important vow he'd ever said. "I can't replace them, but I can be your new family."

Her tears fell then. "My parents would have loved you."

He kissed the wetness away. "And I love you."

She stood up and held a hand out to him. "Let's go upstairs and start that new life."

And they did.

* * * * *

SUSPENSE

Harlequin

INTRIGUE

COMING NEXT MONTH
AVAILABLE JUNE 12, 2012

#1353 WRANGLED
Whitehorse, Montana: Chisholm Cattle Company
B.J. Daniels

#1354 HIGH NOON
Colby, TX
Debra Webb

#1355 EYEWITNESS
Guardians of Coral Cove
Carol Ericson

#1356 DEATH OF A BEAUTY QUEEN
The Delancey Dynasty
Mallory Kane

#1357 THUNDER HORSE HERITAGE
Elle James

#1358 SPY HARD
Dana Marton

REQUEST YOUR FREE BOOKS!
2 FREE NOVELS PLUS 2 FREE GIFTS!

Harlequin®

INTRIGUE®

BREATHTAKING ROMANTIC SUSPENSE

YES! Please send me 2 FREE Harlequin Intrigue® novels and my 2 FREE gifts (gifts are worth about $10). After receiving them, if I don't wish to receive any more books, I can return the shipping statement marked "cancel." If I don't cancel, I will receive 6 brand-new novels every month and be billed just $4.49 per book in the U.S. or $5.24 per book in Canada. That's a saving of at least 14% off the cover price! It's quite a bargain! Shipping and handling is just 50¢ per book in the U.S. and 75¢ per book in Canada.* I understand that accepting the 2 free books and gifts places me under no obligation to buy anything. I can always return a shipment and cancel at any time. Even if I never buy another book, the two free books and gifts are mine to keep forever.

182/382 HDN FEQ2

Name _____ (PLEASE PRINT)

Address _____ Apt. #

City _____ State/Prov. _____ Zip/Postal Code

Signature (if under 18, a parent or guardian must sign)

Mail to the **Reader Service:**
IN U.S.A.: P.O. Box 1867, Buffalo, NY 14240-1867
IN CANADA: P.O. Box 609, Fort Erie, Ontario L2A 5X3

Not valid for current subscribers to Harlequin Intrigue books.

Are you a subscriber to Harlequin Intrigue books
and want to receive the larger-print edition?
Call 1-800-873-8635 or visit www.ReaderService.com.

* Terms and prices subject to change without notice. Prices do not include applicable taxes. Sales tax applicable in N.Y. Canadian residents will be charged applicable taxes. Offer not valid in Quebec. This offer is limited to one order per household. All orders subject to credit approval. Credit or debit balances in a customer's account(s) may be offset by any other outstanding balance owed by or to the customer. Please allow 4 to 6 weeks for delivery. Offer available while quantities last.

Your Privacy—The Reader Service is committed to protecting your privacy. Our Privacy Policy is available online at www.ReaderService.com or upon request from the Reader Service.

We make a portion of our mailing list available to reputable third parties that offer products we believe may interest you. If you prefer that we not exchange your name with third parties, or if you wish to clarify or modify your communication preferences, please visit us at www.ReaderService.com/consumerschoice or write to us at Reader Service Preference Service, P.O. Box 9062, Buffalo, NY 14269. Include your complete name and address.

HI11B

*Harlequin® Romantic Suspense presents the final book
in the gripping PERFECT, WYOMING miniseries
from best-loved veteran series author Carla Cassidy*

*Witness as mercenary Micah Grayson and cult escapee
Olivia Conner join forces to save a little boy and to take
down a monster, while desire explodes between them....*

*Read on for an excerpt from
MERCENARY'S PERFECT MISSION*

Available June 2012 from Harlequin® Romantic Suspense.

"**I** won't tell," she exclaimed fervently. "Please don't hurt me. I swear I won't tell anyone what I saw. Just let me have my other son and we'll go far away from here. I'll never speak your name again." Her voice cracked as she focused on his gun and he realized she believed he was Samuel.

Certainly it was dark enough that it would be easy for anyone to mistake him for his brother. When the brothers were together it was easy to see the subtle differences between them. Micah's face was slightly thinner, his features more chiseled than those of his brother.

At the moment Micah knew Samuel kept his hair cut neat and tidy, while Micah's long hair was tied back. He reached up and pulled the rawhide strip, allowing his hair to fall from its binding.

The woman gasped once again. "You aren't him...but you look like him. Who are you?" Her voice still held fear as she dropped the stick and protectively clutched the baby closer to her chest.

"Who are you?" he countered. He wasn't about to be taken in by a pale-haired angel with big green eyes in this evil place where angels probably couldn't exist.

HRSEXP0612

"I'm Olivia Conner, and this is my son Sam." Tears filled her eyes. "I have another son, but he's still in town. I couldn't get to him before I ran away. I've heard rumors that there was a safe house somewhere, but I've been in the woods for two days and I can't find it."

Micah was unmoved by her tears and by her story. He knew how devious his brother could be, and Micah would do everything possible to protect the location of the safe house. There was only one way to know for sure if she was one of Samuel's "devotees."

Will Olivia be able to get her son back from the clutches of evil? Or will Micah's maniacal twin put an end to them all? Find out in the shocking conclusion to the PERFECT, WYOMING *miniseries.*

MERCENARY'S PERFECT MISSION
Available June 2012, only from
Harlequin® Romantic Suspense, wherever books are sold.

Harlequin®

SPECIAL EDITION

Life, Love and Family

USA TODAY bestselling author

Marie Ferrarella

enchants readers in

ONCE UPON A MATCHMAKER

Micah Muldare's aunt is worried that her nephew
is going to wind up alone in his old age...but this
matchmaking mama has just the thing! When Micah
finds himself accused of theft, defense lawyer
Tracy Ryan agrees to help him as a favor to his aunt,
but soon finds herself drawn to more than just his
case. Will Micah open up his heart and realize
Tracy is his match?

Available June 2012

Saddle up with Harlequin® series books this summer
and find a cowboy for every mood!

Available wherever books are sold.

www.Harlequin.com

HSE65674

Harlequin® Blaze™
red-hot reads

Fall under the spell of fan-favorite author

Leslie Kelly

Workaholic Mimi Burdette thinks she's satisfied dating the handsome man her father has picked out for her. But when sexy firefighter Xander McKinley moves into her apartment building, Mimi finds herself becoming…distracted. When Mimi opens a fortune cookie predicting who will be the man of her dreams, then starts having erotic dreams, she never imagines Xander is having the same dreams! Until they come together and bring those dreams to life.

Blazing Midsummer Nights

The magic begins June 2012

Saddle up with Harlequin® series books this summer and find a cowboy for every mood!

Available wherever books are sold.